A kid in a white mask walked under one of the street lamps on the left. . . .

The parking lot wasn't deserted!

Alex ducked, then raised herself just enough to peer outside. Another small, dark figure was walking right toward her. An orange lightning bolt and a black mask were clearly visible as Bobby Barnswell walked into a circle of light. He was holding a small, black box with a green light.

The GC 161 detector!

Alex ducked again and stayed ducked. When Bobby walked by the family car, the GC 161 in her system would trigger the device and the light would turn red.

The kid would have his witch.

Vince and Danielle would have their GC 161 accident victim.

And life as a normal junior-high kid would be lost to Alex forever. . . .

The Secret World of Alex Mack™

Alex, You're Glowing!
Bet You Can't!
Bad News Babysitting!
Witch Hunt!
Mistaken Identity!
Cleanup Catastrophe!
Take a Hike!
Go for the Gold!

Available from MINSTREL Books

NICKELODEON®

the secret world of

ALEX MACK™

Witch Hunt!

Diana G. Gallagher

A MINSTREL®
BOOK

Published by POCKET BOOKS
New York   London   Toronto   Sydney   Tokyo   Singapore

This book is a work of fiction. Names, characters, places and incidents are products of the author's imagination or are used fictiously. Any resemblance to actual events or locales or persons, living or dead, is entirely coincidental.

A MINSTREL PAPERBACK *Original*

 A Minstrel Book published by
POCKET BOOKS, a division of Simon & Schuster Inc.
1230 Avenue of the Americas, New York, NY 10020

Copyright © 1995 by Viacom International Inc., and RHI Entertainment, Inc. All rights reserved. Based on the Nickelodeon series entitled "The Secret World of Alex Mack."

ISBN: 0-671-53301-0

First Minstrel Books printing October 1995

10 9 8 7 6 5 4 3

NICKELODEON and all related titles, logos and characters are trademarks of Viacom International, Inc.

A MINSTREL BOOK and colophon are registered trademarks of Simon & Schuster Inc.

Cover photography by Thomas Queally and Danny Feld

Printed in the U.S.A.

For Donna Bozgan,
an enthusiastic friend and
most excellent research assistant

Witch Hunt!

CHAPTER 1

"Hurry up, Raymond," Alex called impatiently. "Robyn and Nicole are waiting for us, and I don't want to miss the beginning of the movie!"

Raymond Alvarado ran to join Alex and her sister, Annie Mack, on the sidewalk. "Sorry," he said breathlessly. Holding up a rubber mask of an ugly alien creature, Raymond fell into step between the girls. "It took me forever to find this mask."

"What a waste of time, Raymond," Alex said. "You don't need a mask—you're scary enough as it is." Raymond was Alex's next-door neighbor and best friend as well.

1

Raymond held the mask up on his face and, sticking his tongue through the mouth hole, loomed in front of Alex while making a growling monster noise. "Is that scary enough for you?" he said after he lowered the mask.

"It is pretty nasty, Ray," Alex said. "Are you wearing it to the Halloween party tonight?" The company Alex's father worked for, Paradise Valley Chemical, was throwing a Halloween party, and the whole town was invited.

"No way!" Lifting his chin, Raymond squared his shoulders and struck a dignified pose. "I'm going to the party in style."

"As what?" Annie asked, raising a skeptical eyebrow. "No, wait. Let me guess. The surfing zombie of Malibu Beach, sporting color-coordinated Baggies and board that complement your grotesque green, rotting flesh?"

Alex giggled. Every Halloween Raymond's costume got grosser and more outrageous. Last year he had smeared green slime over the alien mask for a more realistic effect.

"Get real, Annie," Raymond said. "I'm through with that kid stuff. I'd rather dance with girls—not gross them out."

Alex understood exactly how he felt. They were

in junior high now. She was going to the plant party as a gypsy, wearing makeup instead of a childish mask.

"Whoa, cool!" Raymond pointed to a house on the corner. A life-size scarecrow sat in a rocking chair on its porch, and a ghost suspended from the overhang fluttered in the breeze. Gobs of fake spider webs were stretched between the pillars.

"We're late, Ray," Alex said, giving him a nudge. She glanced at the old witch mask she was carrying. The stringy, gray hair attached to the edge was coming unglued, and the hard plastic was cracked, but Annie had insisted they all wear full face masks to the monster movie matinee. Worse, Annie had insisted on going.

"I hate to admit it, Raymond," Annie said, "but Halloween just won't seem the same without your warped determination to reach new heights of nauseating tastelessness every year."

Sometimes Alex got a little tired of listening to all the big words her older sister used. *Why can't she just say it the easy way?* Alex thought. She could have just said "Raymond is usually a total gross out on Halloween." But instead Annie gave them a mini-vocabulary lesson every chance she got. Annie was a scientific genius, like Mr. Mack, and she got A's in all subjects without even trying. Alex had to try a little harder—no, a lot harder—to get those kinds of marks. She and Annie shared a bedroom, but sometimes Alex thought that was about all they had in common.

"Yeah. I'm going to miss trick-or-treating." Raymond sighed wistfully, then grinned. "Although I still might be able to come up with a few tricks tonight."

"You're not planning to toilet-paper the plant parking lot or anything else equally stupid, are you?" Annie asked Raymond suspiciously.

"Now, that's not such a bad idea," Alex said. Thanks to the chemical company, her life hadn't been the same since she had almost been run down by one of their trucks and drenched in an experimental compound called GC 161. The gold liquid had changed her so she could move things with her mind, shoot out electrical charges from her fingers, and transform into a puddle of ooze at will. And when she morphed into the slippery gel, she could ooze herself anywhere she wanted to go—even under closed doors and through tiny keyholes.

"Forget it, Alex." Raymond held up his hands. "I don't want any trouble with Danielle Atron's security guys, especially that Vince. He is one mean dude."

"That's the truth." Alex felt chilled just thinking about Vince. He was the head of plant security and determined to find the GC 161 accident victim. And his boss, Danielle Atron, was even more determined.

Annie paused to stare at a display of cardboard tombstones on a lawn. "If Danielle Atron finds out you're the kid, Alex, you'll be worse then dead. You'll vanish into the plant labs. Poof! Never to be seen again."

"I know that, Annie. You don't have to keep reminding me." How could she possibly forget? Ever since she had been drenched with the GC 161, Alex had to be supercareful that no one ever found out. The driver of the truck, a guy named Dave, hadn't gotten a good look at her that day. But the plant was determined to find her, since the chemical was an illegal gene-altering compound. What they didn't know was that it gave Alex some really strange powers. And if they knew that, who knew what they'd do to Alex to make sure that she never went to the authorities about the illegal substance? Another thing that scared Alex was that her father could lose his job if anything happened to the plant. So she kept her secret to herself. Her sister and Ray were the only ones who knew. Not even Nicole and Robyn knew—it was safer for them if they didn't.

"Come to think of it, though," Raymond said, "we haven't seen much of Vince or that Dave guy lately."

"Maybe because they're not looking for me any more," Alex said hopefully.

"And maybe they're deliberately laying off to give us a false sense of security. You know Danielle Atron will never give up." Annie took a crumpled cat mask out of her back pocket and wrinkled her nose. "Why am I doing this?"

"Yeah. Why are you?" Raymond asked. "One of the movies is *Frankenstein,* and you hate movies about mad scientists."

Annie shrugged. "I have my reasons."

"Like what?" Raymond pressed.

Annie hesitated, then shrugged again. "Alex wants to go."

"I'm not gonna pass up free movies and a good time just because you worry too much, Annie."

"What's to worry about?" Raymond asked, puzzled.

"Annie thinks the matinee might be a trap,"

Alex whispered, "because Paradise Valley Chemical is giving every kid in town a free pass to it."

"Better safe than sorry," Annie said.

"It's just for public relations," Alex said defensively. Their mother, Barbara Mack, was in charge of Paradise Valley Chemical's public relations account. Danielle Atron never missed an opportunity to promote the company throughout the community. The free Halloween movie was just another plant-sponsored event.

"Just like the party at the plant tonight. No big deal, right?" Raymond asked.

"Maybe." Annie frowned thoughtfully. "Personally, I'd rather stay home and read than go to a company party with my parents, but they said Alex and I have to go."

"Yeah, same with my dad." Raymond shook his head. His father worked for the plant too. "How's a party animal supposed to impress the girls if he's there with his dad?"

Annie wasn't listening to Raymond's problems. Instead she fixed Alex with a penetrating stare and said, "If I see anything in the theater that looks even remotely suspicious, we're out of there."

"Annie, we're just going to the movies!" Alex exclaimed. *Raymond thinks he has problems!* she thought. *Try having an older sister like Annie.* Sometimes Alex felt like she had *three* parents.

Annie crossed her arms and set her jaw.

"Actually, she's got a good point, Alex," Raymond said. "Chances are this is just a movie and not something Danielle Atron cooked up to catch you. But on the other hand, what if it is a trap?"

"Why do you always agree with Annie, Raymond?"

"I make sense, that's why," Annie said before Raymond could open his mouth. "Why are you always arguing with me when I'm only trying to protect you?"

Alex sagged. "I don't know, Annie. Honest. It just seems like I can't do anything without having to worry about someone finding out I've got these stupid powers."

"They're not stupid, Alex," Raymond said. "They're totally cool. I'm the only guy in school whose best friend can turn into jello and start a dead battery without jumper cables. It's radical."

"He's right for once, Alex," Annie said. "Nobody else I know has a sister who can turn a room full of ordinary objects into a fleet of UFOs." Annie smiled. "I just don't want something awful to happen to you."

"Right." Although Alex appreciated Annie's concern, her sister's overly protective paranoia was starting to spoil everything Alex wanted to do for fun. But Alex was determined that today would be different. She'd go to the theater, get some delicious buttered popcorn and a soda, and have a great time.

Vince's ear itched under the black visored helmet that covered his face and head, but he didn't dare remove the mask to scratch. Too many of the local teens knew him by sight. The worst thing he could do was to alert the kid who had been exposed to GC 161 that the head of Paradise Valley Chemical security was in the theater. In his black plastic armor over a black turtleneck, with high boots and a long cape, Vince smiled in anticipation. The futuristic soldier costume was an uncomfortable but appropriate disguise. By the end of the afternoon, he would successfully identify the kid affected by GC 161.

"Which button do I push again, Vince?" Dressed as a clown, Dave held out a small black device that looked like a remote control for a TV. Bright orange hair fringed his bald head, and a bewildered frown was hidden by the red smile painted on his white face. A red ball pinched his nose, giving his voice a muffled, nasal sound.

Vince quickly moved in front of Dave to block the device from view. They were working under-cover as ushers for the free movies, and his dim-witted partner was about to blow it. Dave had been driving the Paradise Valley Chemical truck that spilled GC 161 on the unknown kid. And as a secu-rity partner, Vince thought that Dave not only caused accidents, he was an accident about to hap-pen at any moment. Although he hadn't gotten a good look at the victim, Dave was the only witness, so Vince was stuck working with him.

"Where are the flowers I gave you?" Vince hissed.

"Right here." Dave held up the bouquet of large, fake red flowers with floppy, green leaves clutched in his other hand.

"Put the detector inside the bouquet," Vince or-dered softly.

Dave glanced between the flowers and the de-vice, then blinked. "Huh?"

"It belongs in the—never mind. Give it to me." Snatching the flowers from Dave, Vince snapped the device into a plastic holder nestled in the mid-dle of the bouquet. The flowers hid the device, but

Dave could still see the readout by looking down from above. "It's part of your costume, understand?"

Dave hesitated, then grinned. "Oh. I thought we were supposed to be scanning the kids for GC 161."

"We *are*, you idiot!" Vince waved an identical device in Dave's perplexed face.

The compact GC 161 detectors had been designed by the plant laboratory to register traces of the experimental chemical. If the kid came within ten feet of the scanner, the green light would react to the presence of the potent compound and flash red.

"I'll explain this one more time, Dave," Vince said in a pained voice. "We're in costume so we won't be recognized. The detectors have to look like part of the costumes so the kids won't know we're scanning them." Vince clipped his device to his belt, then stepped back and shrugged the cape over his shoulders. The black detector went perfectly with his black disguise. "See?"

Dave nodded. "Got it, but which button do I push?"

A mob of costumed teens were waiting outside, and the theater manager was about to open the outer doors. Vince dragged Dave across the lobby, stationed him by one of two entrances, then activated his GC 161 detector.

"Don't push anything, Dave." Vince flipped a clip over the depressed button on Dave's detector to hold it in place. A green light flashed on. "Just keep it aimed at the kids as they file by and watch the light. If it turns red, call me."

"Okay." Dave sniffed as the aroma of freshly popped and buttered popcorn filled the air. "Can I grab a snack?"

"No!" Vince pointed toward the outer doors.

Dozens of laughing kids swarmed into the lobby.

Vince activated his own device and hurried to the other entrance. Most of the teenagers were wearing alien, animal, or monster masks. Those who looked more human dressed as punks, bikers, hippies, and bums were lost in the crush. Vince couldn't positively identify anyone, not by sight. But when the GC 161 victim walked by, the green light would turn red and the hunt would be over.

Just before they turned the corner onto the main avenue, Annie stopped and pressed her face against the bookstore window. "It's about time!"

she exclaimed. "I've been waiting for that book to come out for weeks."

Alex peered in the window over Annie's shoulder. Orange and red autumn leaves, pumpkins, and fold-out bats were arranged around numerous Halloween books. "Which one?" Alex said. "*The Witches Of Spook High* or *Betsey's Best Costume Ever?* A little below your accelerated reading level, aren't they?"

Annie pointed. "*The Order of Chaos.* On the shelf over there. It's a definitive study of chaos theory in relation to a multi-universe system."

"Of course." Rolling her eyes, Alex thought, *How boring!* When Annie was three and they asked her what she wanted to be when she grew up, Annie actually said a chemical engineer. *Sometimes I wonder if we're even related*, Alex mused.

Alex looked over at the window filled with children's books. Hand on his chin, Raymond was studying several jack-o'-lanterns carved by elementary school kids. Blue, red, and yellow prize ribbons were tacked to the winners in the contest.

"Come on, you guys!" Alex urged. "I hate getting to a movie late."

"What difference does it make, Alex," Annie

said. "You've seen *Frankenstein* and *Dracula* dozens of times on TV."

"They've added some stuff they took out in 1931," Raymond said.

"And there's no commercials," Alex called over her shoulder as she jogged around the corner and stopped abruptly. The sidewalk in front of the theater was deserted. "Great. Everybody's inside. Now we'll have to stumble around in the dark looking for seats."

"If there are any seats left." Raymond sighed.

Glancing at her watch, Alex quickened her pace. "It's only five after. Maybe it hasn't started yet."

"Masks!" Annie ordered.

"Okay." Unfolding the battered witch mask, Alex put it on.

Raymond slipped his alien mask on, tucked the plastic flaps under his collar, and snapped to attention. "Ready, sir."

Donning the cat mask, Annie sighed. "I can't believe I'm going to a monster movie wearing a plastic cat face."

Alex didn't want her older sister tagging along. She wanted to sit with her friends and laugh and scream and throw popcorn without Annie around to disapprove of her "typical adolescent behavior."

Having Annie as a watchdog was really starting to cramp her style.

As if she could read Alex's mind, Annie tugged on her sleeve and said, "Remember, be careful in there."

"Chill, Annie," Alex said. "It's just a movie."

CHAPTER 2

Just inside the entrance to the theater, Dave stared at the detector in his hand, mesmerized by the green light.

"Dave," Vince said, tapping the truck driver on the shoulder.

"What?" Startled, Dave jumped and his red nose popped off. "Oh, it's you, Vince. You scared me. Are we done? The movie's about to start."

"No, we're not done. More kids could still arrive. I've got to go to the men's room for a minute," Vince said tightly. "You stay here just in case someone comes in late. Wander between the two doors. Look casual."

16

"Why?" Dave picked up his fallen nose, stuck it back on, and raised the detector. "No red light. The kid we want isn't here."

"Exactly." Sighing heavily, Vince turned, then looked back. "Do *not* leave this lobby."

"Okay."

Bored, Dave strolled to the far wall, did an about-face, and strolled back. The movie's creepy opening music was drowned out by loud cheering and whoops from the teenaged audience, but not the noisy grumbling in Dave's stomach.

Two kids approached the counter and the first ordered a large popcorn. Fishing into his clown suit pocket, Dave pulled out a wad of crumpled dollar bills and glanced toward the men's room. Vince would be back any minute, but he simply couldn't stand it any longer. He was hungry, and the smell of roasted peanuts and buttered popcorn was driving him crazy.

So what if Vince yells at me, Dave thought. Vince was always yelling at him.

After placing the bouquet in the ticket stand by the doorway, Dave walked over to the candy counter and stood in line.

*   *   *

Alex pushed through the glass doors into the old theater and paused to glance around. This was her favorite theater in town—the old fashioned kind—and she knew it well. The crystal chandelier still hung from the high, domed ceiling. Tall, gold pillars carved with elaborate designs stood in the corners. Heavy drapes and classic movie posters adorned the walls around glass cases filled with movie memorabilia. The building was a replica of an old movie house in Danielle Atron's hometown. She had built the single-screen theater in Paradise Valley as a monument to the golden days of movies past.

As the outer doors closed behind them, Annie and Raymond fell silent, too. The museum-like interior of the ornate lobby seemed to demand quiet. Even the hushed rumble of the crowd and the strains of weird music that drifted in from the theater were muted by the heavy curtains and thick carpeting.

Alex was heading for the snack counter just as her sister said, "No time for junk food. Let's go find seats."

Alex grumbled as she followed Annie and Raymond to the doorway leading into the theater. There were a couple of kids and a clown buying popcorn at the candy counter. She'd have to go back during intermission for her popcorn. The carpet muffled the sound of footsteps, and neither the clown nor the cashier noticed Alex, Annie and Raymond tiptoe past.

"It's pitch black in here!" Raymond whispered loudly as he stepped through the drapes. "Ow! That's my foot, Annie!"

"Sorry, Raymond," Annie apologized absently as she scanned the dark interior. "I can't see anything!"

"Looking for someone?" Alex paused between the drapes, letting the lobby light filter through so they could see.

"Who? Me?" Annie responded shortly, as though the very idea was ridiculous. "Of course not."

"Good thing," Alex said. The theater was dark and packed. Robyn and Nicole were there somewhere, but she didn't expect to find them. On the screen, Dr. Frankenstein and Igor were lifting a coffin out of a grave.

Alex shivered, suddenly feeling as though some ghostly presence had crawled across her skin. She glanced back. The clown was still chatting with the candy girl and no one else was in sight. A blinking red light in a bunch of fake flowers on the ticket stand caught Alex's eye as she let the curtains fall.

Just Halloween jitters, Alex decided as her eyes grew accustomed to the dark. The old movie theater was a perfect setting for a chilling afternoon of monster movies.

"Yo, dorky Doc Frank-en-stein!" Someone in the audience hollered. "Igor. Igor. Igor."

Everyone immediately took up the chant and began stamping their feet, clapping their hands, and whooping.

"Down there!" Raymond yelled to be heard above the din. "I see three seats in the third row on the left."

"After you," Annie said, grabbing Raymond's shirttail. Then she reached back and took Alex's hand. "You owe me for this one."

"No way!" Alex laughed as she let Annie haul her blindly down the aisle. "You volunteered. I didn't invite you."

"Hey, Alex? Is that you?"

Recognizing Scott's voice, Alex stopped and pushed her mask up. Scott was not only the coolest, cutest boy she had ever met, he was the nicest, too. He was also friendly with the pretty and athletic, but not quite so nice, Kelly. The older girl despised Alex because Scott always said hello to her. Alex couldn't help liking him . . . a lot.

Scott waved from the middle of the theater. Kelly wasn't with him, but every seat in the center row was taken. *Just my luck,* Alex thought, blushing as she waved back and said, "Hi, Scott! How ya doin'?"

"Great. You goin' to the plant party tonight?"

"Everyone's going to the party tonight, Scott!" The boy sitting beside him cuffed him on the arm. "So pipe down!"

"I'll be there!" Alex whispered back as loud as she could as Annie yanked her hand.

Kelly was probably home getting ready for the big costume event, Alex figured, and she was sure to wear something spectacular. Alex was glad she had decided to go as a gypsy. Even Annie thought she looked good in the colorful costume.

A shower of popcorn pelted them from behind.

"Why didn't I stay home," Annie groaned.

"Good question," Alex mumbled.

"Yo! Lou!" Raymond hooted to someone seated near the aisle. A boy Alex knew from English class held out a hand and Raymond slapped it as he passed by. "Later, dude."

"I thought you were mad at Louis because he

went out with Natalie Hobbs last week," Alex teased. Raymond had had a secret crush on Natalie for a month.

"I was." Raymond grinned. "It turned out to be the *worst* night of his life. She giggled through the whole movie, then talked nonstop about cheerleading at Burger Castle later."

"Down in front!" The call echoed through the theater.

Hunkering down, Alex and Annie scurried behind Raymond to the third row.

"It's about time!" Seated in the second row, Nicole looked back. "Do you have any idea how hard it is to save three seats at a free double feature on a Saturday afternoon?"

"That just happens to be Halloween?" Robyn added. "The odds against success are astronomical."

"How'd you manage it?" Alex asked as she climbed over a guy sitting at the end of the row. She sat next to him so she could be close to Robyn and Nicole.

"We had help from King Kong back there." Nicole nodded toward the older boy next to Alex. Alex glanced over and noticed that he was wearing a gorilla mask.

"A lucky break for us, huh?" Alex said.

"I don't think luck had anything to do with it," Robyn said.

"Sorry." Annie sighed as she stumbled over the boy in the gorilla mask. The string on her old cat mask broke, and it fell into his lap.

"No problem, Annie." The boy took off his mask and grinned.

"Jason! You're here!" Annie said, sounding surprised.

"I said I'd be here, and I'm a man of my word."

Alex moved over so her sister could sit next to the boy. "Friend of yours, Annie?"

"New kid in school. Jason Andrews. He's a major whiz in chemistry."

Robyn and Nicole exchanged knowing glances and giggled.

"Uh-huh." Alex wasn't fooled for a minute, either. No wonder Annie had insisted on hanging out with her at the movies. All that talk about a trap was just an excuse. Annie had come to see Jason. "He's really cute, Annie," Alex whispered, "for a gorilla."

"Watch the movie, Alex."

Grinning, Alex concentrated on the screen.

*   *   *

Vince couldn't believe his eyes.

Red! The light on Dave's detector was flashing red!

"You don't have to stand there, Vince," Dave said as he ambled toward the front entrance, popcorn under an arm. "I've got it covered." He shoved two candy bars into his pocket.

"Who came in?" Vince demanded.

"Nobody." Dave glanced at the flowers in the ticket stand and almost choked on a mouthful of popcorn. "It's red."

"Yes, it is, Dave. It's flashing red. You're very observant." Vince's voice was strained and dripped with sarcasm.

"I didn't see anyone, Vince. Honest."

"Someone set this thing off while you were stuffing your face, and we're going to find out who." Taking the flashing detector out of the bouquet, Vince reset it to green and slapped it into Dave's hand. "Now!"

"But I gotta—"

"Now." Fuming, Vince pointed through the left doorway. "You take that aisle. I'll take the one on the right. We're gonna find that kid." Vince pressed close to Dave, looked him in the eye, and spoke in a softer, yet more menacing tone. "Do we understand each other?"

"I'll go left." Setting down the popcorn bucket on the counter, Dave went through the drapes without another word.

Taking a deep breath to calm himself, Vince headed down the right aisle. The GC 161 accident kid was in the theater, and the detector would find the kid, wherever he or she was.

This time, there would be no way out.

CHAPTER 3

Alex took off her witch mask and settled back to enjoy the movie. Annie was sitting ramrod straight beside her, pretending *not* to be interested in Jason Andrews.

"Where's your mask?" Annie whispered. She was worried that someone from the plant might somehow figure out who her sister really was.

"In my lap," Alex hissed back. "I can't see through those little tiny holes!"

"Neither can I." Raymond peeled off his mask and inhaled deeply. "Much better. Could hardly breathe, either."

"At least you didn't slime it this time." Nicole shuddered.

"I ran out," Raymond said. "But maybe I'll try ketchup today."

Robyn glanced back. "Give me a break."

Alex laughed. Last year Robyn had spent all Halloween night trying to get the sticky, green goop out of her long, red hair.

"Just keep the mask handy." Annie whispered in Alex's ear, then stiffened as Jason edged closer and set his popcorn cup on the chair arm between them.

"Want some, Annie?" he offered.

"Uh—sure. Thanks." Annie took a handful and shifted ever so slightly closer to Jason.

On the screen, Igor broke the beaker that had the normal brain in it and stole the abnormal, criminal brain.

"How classically camp," Jason said. "I love it." He and Annie both laughed, appreciating the movie's absurd science.

Alex grinned, but it wasn't the movie that made her smile. Annie dated Bruce Lester occasionally, but he was too busy with his studies at Phillipsburg Academy to visit very often. *But*, Alex realized, *if Annie had a steady, local boyfriend, she might leave me alone!*

"Excuse me, Alex." Raymond stood up.

"Where are you going, Ray? We just got here."

"This is a slow part, and I can't sit through a movie without something to eat. Popcorn or nachos?"

"Both." Alex drew her legs up so he could get by.

On the screen Elizabeth was telling Henry that she was worried about her fiancé, Victor Frankenstein.

Not exactly exciting, Alex thought. However, Jason casually draped his arm over the back of Annie's seat. Annie tensed, but she didn't ask him to remove it.

Now that's interesting, Alex decided, looking at the two out of the corner of her eye. She focused back on the screen, keeping her fingers crossed that Jason's interest would last a lot longer than the double feature.

Alex's stomach growled, and she looked up the aisle, wishing Raymond would hurry with the munchies. She saw that Raymond *was* on his way back—in a hurry, but empty-handed. *What?* she thought, *no popcorn?*

"What's with you, Raymond?" Annie asked as Raymond stumbled back to his seat.

As he crawled past Alex, he stepped on her foot. "Don't panic, okay?" Raymond whispered as he groped for his seat and then sat down. Wide-eyed and frantic, he looked like he had seen a ghost.

Alex was beginning to think this was about more than a popcorn shortage.

"Who's gonna panic?" Nicole turned in her seat to scowl at him. "It's just a movie. So what's the problem?"

"Problem?" Raymond's head jerked up. "No problem." He sat stiffly, smiling tightly until Nicole shrugged and turned back toward the screen.

Alex's hands started to sweat.

"What's wrong, Raymond?" Annie leaned across Alex's lap.

"I'm not sure, okay, but I think we've got big trouble. That clown and another dude dressed like a sci-fi guy are coming down the aisles with these little black gizmos. Like they're looking for something, you know?"

"Or someone?" Annie chanced a glance back and inhaled sharply. "Uh-oh."

"Uh-oh?" Alex froze in her seat.

"Yeah. Exactly," Raymond said softly. "Black gizmos with green lights. Suspicious, huh?"

"Green lights?" Alex gasped softly. She had seen a flashing *red* light in the clown's flowers. What did it mean?

Robyn looked back with a worried frown. "You sure everything's okay?"

"Fine!" Alex said quickly.

"Just fine." Raymond nodded emphatically.

"Will you guys shut up!" The girl in the row behind them kicked the back of Alex's chair.

"Chill out," Raymond snapped in a forced whisper.

"What's the matter, Annie?" Jason asked.

"Nothing, Jason." Annie turned sideways to block Jason's view of Alex and Raymond.

Alex slid farther down in her seat and glanced over her shoulder. The clown was moving slowly down the aisle, holding the bouquet. Even though he was trying to shield it with his hand, she could see a green glow emerge.

"Do you think it's them?" Raymond asked Annie.

"Vince and Dave?" Annie said. "I wouldn't be surprised."

"It's them. I know it's them!" Alex said. She was

beginning to panic, the worst thing she could do. She glowed when she got really nervous, and right now she felt an all-too-familiar flushed feeling on her skin.

"They've got something that can identify me," Alex said grimly. "I just know it. The light was red and now—"

"Oh, no!" Annie grabbed the witch mask out of Alex's lap, shoved it over her face, then adjusted the elastic to keep it in place. "You're glowing again," she said in Alex's ear. "You've got to get out of here."

"How am I supposed to do that?" Alex tucked her shining, golden hands under her armpits. At least she was wearing long sleeves and jeans.

"Morph and go under the seats. There's no other way."

The movie screen faded into the dark image of Frankenstein's castle. Thunder boomed and lightning cracked as the mad scientist prepared to bring the monster to life in his lab.

The girl behind them bent forward. "You guys are really making me mad."

Alex slid down until she was almost lying on the seat.

"Better back off," Raymond told the girl. "I think

I'm gonna be sick." He heaved slightly and made a disgusting noise for good measure. The girl couldn't sit back fast enough.

"Not on me, you don't!" Robyn ducked and shot Raymond a withering glance before turning forward again.

Alex buried her face against Annie's arm just in case the glow was visible through the eyes holes and around the edges of the mask. She had to get out of there now. The chance that Robyn and Nicole might turn around and notice the strange, golden gleam in her eyes or see her change into a puddle was making her even more anxious. The glow intensified.

Raymond sat forward and draped his arms over Robyn and Nicole's seats. "This is the best part," he said, trying to keep their attention off Alex.

"We know, Raymond," Nicole said.

"Is something wrong?" Jason asked Annie with a troubled frown. "Anything I can do to help?"

"No, everything's fine." Annie took Jason's hand to distract him. "Are you going to the plant party tonight?"

"Yeah. Being new on the job, my dad figures it can't hurt to show up and impress the top banana. Are you?"

"Probably," Annie said coyly. "My parents have worked for the plant forever, but they wouldn't dream of not going, either. Danielle Atron *will* notice who's there and who's not, believe me."

If Alex hadn't been so scared, she would have laughed. Annie was actually making a play for a boy. Even though she was doing it so Jason wouldn't see her sister turn into a puddle of ooze, Alex was pretty sure Annie didn't mind. Not one bit.

However, Alex had other things to worry about, like getting out of the theater without being seen. She wasn't *absolutely* positive that the clown and space soldier were using some new kind of GC 161 device to search the theater, but she couldn't afford to assume differently. It was time to focus on morphing.

A warm prickling started in Alex's toes, then surged through every cell in her body as she transformed. The sensation was like sliding into a tub of hot water except that she *became* the water. One second she was solid. Then muscle and bone turned to jellied mush.

"Hurry, Alex." Raymond sat back and hissed softly. "They're almost here."

Oozing between the seats, Alex quickly slithered

under Raymond's seat. She paused a second, gathered herself, then raced for her life along the wall. She could only hope that everyone was too engrossed in the movie to notice the silvery stream of glop speeding toward the back of the theater.

All her senses were heightened by the threat of imminent capture, and Alex was aware of everything that happened in the next several seconds.

A boy at the end of the row had one foot on the floor touching the wall. Alex was going so fast, she slithered over his boot before she could slow down to avoid it.

"What was that?" The boy jumped to his feet.

Another girl shrieked as Alex shot by. "It's the blob!"

The clown screamed at the same time. "Vince! Vince! Over here! It's red!"

"Don't anybody move!" Vince shouted.

A nervous hush fell over the theater as Alex scooted along the back wall. Just before she slid behind the drapes over the entrance, she saw Vince run up to Dave. The truck driver was standing by the third row where Annie and Raymond were still sitting. The flowers no longer glowed with a green light. They were flashing red.

Alex was positive now. The black device could

detect GC 161. The free movie was a trap, just as Annie had feared.

Stunned by how close she had come to getting caught, Alex didn't stick around to find out what would happen next. Hidden by the drapes, she moved along the edge of the lobby, then paused to figure out the best escape route.

A short hallway connected the lobby to an emergency exit on the side of the building. The long curtains would conceal her all the way to the door. She began oozing along the wall toward the hallway.

"Hey!" A young voice yelled. He was only a few feet away from Alex.

"Be quiet!" A feminine voice ordered. It was the cashier at the candy counter.

Alex realized that the drapes didn't quite reach the floor. She chanced a peek underneath them and saw a boy who looked about eleven. He leaned over to get a better look. His mouth fell open as his gaze found her.

"Hey, lady!" The boy shouted and pointed toward Alex.

"I said be quiet!" The cashier glared at him.

"But there's a big, yucky mess behind those curtains." He looked at the candy clerk. "I'm not kidding, lady!"

The young woman squinted toward the curtains. "I don't see anything, kid. Now be quiet or I'll have the manager throw you out. And I'm not kidding, either." The woman turned away to finish refilling the popcorn machine.

Alex slithered toward the exit while they weren't watching. Once she was in the short hall, she would be out of sight, and, she hoped, out of the boy's mind.

"Gosh! That stuff is moving!" The boy exclaimed.

Alex reached the emergency door and flattened herself even more so she could zip underneath it. But when she tried to slither into the crack, she smashed into a solid barrier.

"Oww!" Squealing in pain, Alex felt herself glob up to the door and smush against it. Dazed, she hesitated a second, then carefully examined the bottom of the door. It was airtight; not even a paper-thin crack would allow her to slip through.

"Where are you going?" Alex heard the candy clerk's voice carry down the hall.

"To check out that icky stuff," the boy answered firmly.

Oh no. He's coming, Alex thought frantically. *I'm trapped!*

CHAPTER 4

Annie tensed as Vince ran up to Dave at the end of her row. Although the two men were standing only a few feet away, she couldn't see them well in the dim light. But she could hear their hushed, but excited voices. Straining to hear what they said, Annie held Jason's hand tighter. Then she noticed that a red light was blinking in the middle of Dave's bouquet.

"Give me that," Vince grabbed the flowers, then reached inside and clicked something. The red light turned green. He stared at the bouquet a moment, then shook it. "You sure it went off right here?" he asked Dave.

"Yep. Right here. The third row." Dave nodded so vigorously, his nose popped off. He fell onto his hands and knees to look for it.

Vince hit the bouquet. "Something's not right . . ."

"Hey, you guys! We can't see!" someone yelled.

A soda cup sailed through the air and hit the back of Vince's helmet. The plastic lid popped off and crushed ice flew everywhere. Vince whirled around, ducking a barrage of popcorn and crumpled paper napkins. The crowd's hoots and squeals forced him to the floor on his knees beside Dave.

"It's gone, Vince," Dave wailed. "I can't find it anywhere!"

"What's gone?" Vince's voice carried as the crowd quieted.

"My nose! I can't find my nose!"

"Forget the nose, Dave. The light is still green. The kid was here but got away somehow."

Annie shook, and Jason's arm tightened around her shoulders. He thought she was cold, but she couldn't explain the real reason she was trembling. Everyone else had turned their attention back to the movie. Only she and Raymond knew what was really going on.

The gizmo was a GC 161 detector, and Alex had triggered it. She had gotten away in time, but the detector could find her again—anywhere, at any time!

Annie didn't dare leave to see if Alex was okay, not just yet anyway. It would look too suspicious.

She made a mental note to remind Raymond to put his mask back on before they left. Vince wasn't stupid. He'd be on the lookout for all the kids that were sitting in the third row.

Don't panic! Think!

Alex huddled behind the curtain, a shivering glob of jelly. The boy was coming to investigate—he'd be here any second! The only way she could get outside was to materialize back to her normal self so she could open the door.

Concentrating, she felt the familiar warm tingle and morphed into herself. The process only took a couple of seconds, but it seemed longer. Time was not on her side. The instant Alex was solid again, she jumped to the emergency door.

In the theater, a thundering chorus of voices shouted along with Dr. Frankenstein. ''It's alive! It's alive!''

Without thinking, Alex looked back to see if the boy had gotten a good look at her. *Big mistake,* she realized too late. Because she was more nervous than ever, Alex was still glowing when she had become solid again. By the expression on the boy's face, she knew for sure that the golden light shone through the holes and cracks in the witch mask.

The boy stopped dead in his tracks and exclaimed, "Holy cow!"

Alex made her break for the outside. As she pushed on the bar and shoved the door open, alarms immediately began to shriek. Now she had much more than a curious boy to worry about. Vince and Dave would hear the alarms and be hot on her heels.

Bursting through the door, Alex found herself in the alley between the theater and a barber shop. The street was to her right, but traffic was heavy and she couldn't get across it.

"Hey! There's a witch out here!" The boy shouted from the other side of the emergency door. Then it slowly began to open.

Alex glanced at her hands and saw that her panicked state was making them glow brighter than ever. *That's no surprise,* Alex thought as she turned left and ran down the alley. She had had some close calls since GC 161 turned her into a teenaged freak, but she had never actually been *chased* before.

The boy shoved through the door and took off after her, screaming at the top of his lungs, "Witch! It's a witch!"

Alex had always sympathized with Frankenstein's monster. He hadn't asked to be brought back to life. Just like she hadn't asked to be doused with GC 161. They were both victims of dangerous scientific experiments, and now she really knew how the monster felt when the townspeople had hunted him down.

Even though she was running from just a kid, it was terrifying.

Alex focused her thoughts on several trash cans by the barber shop. It was hard to concentrate and run at the same time, but she had to slow down the boy somehow. Her telekinetic power engaged, and the trash cans toppled. Then she set them rolling down the narrow alley toward the pursuing kid.

He yelled and ducked out of the way as two of them rolled toward him.

Alex kept running . . . until she came to a six-foot chainlink fence across the end of the alley. There was a gate, but it was padlocked. Alex glanced back and didn't see the boy. Knowing it was safe to use her powers, she zapped the lock.

The electrical charge that flew from her fingers was stronger than usual, maybe because she was so scared. Her zap action didn't just break the padlock. It fried it. The smoking, metal lock fell to the ground in two pieces, and the wire mesh around the latch was sizzling hot.

Pushing through the gate, Alex dashed for a stand of trees by an apartment complex across the narrow, back street. She paused behind a large tree. Breathless and exhausted, she watched as the boy walked up to the gate and stopped.

The boy looked at the ground, then up and down the street. His gaze swept across the dense foliage where she was hiding, but apparently he couldn't see her. Shoulders drooping, he turned and walked back to the theater.

Safe for the moment, Alex sat down to recover her wits and her energy. She wasn't going anywhere for a while. She was still glowing.

When the alarms went off, Vince and Dave ran to the lobby.

Annie waited. It wasn't easy just sitting there, wondering if Alex was all right, but she had to be patient. She didn't want to do anything that would attract Vince's attention.

The moment the alarms fell silent, Annie poked Raymond. "Come on. Let's get out of here."

"But the movie's just starting to get good."

"We have to go find Alex." Annie looked at him pointedly, then put on the awful cat mask.

"Right." Raymond slipped into his alien head. He bumped the back of Nicole's seat as he stood up.

"Up or down, Raymond!" Nicole said sharply. She looked back and frowned. "Where's Alex?"

"Are you leaving?" Jason asked Annie with obvious disappointment.

"Yeah. 'Fraid so." Annie quickly made up an excuse. "Alex was feeling sick, and I want to make sure she got home all right."

"Your sister?" Jason frowned and peered around her. "I thought she was sitting right there?"

"No. She left." Annie jumped up from her seat to avoid any further discussion.

"Alex went home?" Robyn asked incredulously. "After we guarded those seats with our lives?"

"She must be sick," Nicole observed. "The only thing Alex likes better than monster movies is Scott."

"I hope she's all right," Robyn said.

"Me, too," Annie added sincerely, then moved

to squeeze by Jason. "Nice seeing you. Have to go."

"Guess I will, too, then." Jason stood up, blocking Annie's way. "I've seen this movie a hundred times."

"No doubt." Annie followed him out of the row and up the aisle, wondering if he actually liked girls who were marginally rude. She hadn't meant to be so abrupt. She just didn't want to explain Alex's unexplainable vanishing act.

When they reached the lobby, Annie stopped so suddenly, Raymond ran into her. Annie nodded toward the rest rooms. There, Vince and Dave were talking to a grade-school boy who was gesturing wildly with his hands. The kid was excited about something, very excited, Annie realized with a sinking feeling.

"I have to go to the ladies' room, Ray. Be right back," Annie said.

Jason, who had been waiting by the front exit, returned to stand with Raymond.

"You don't have to wait, Jason," Annie said.

"That's okay. I don't have anything else to do right now."

Annie didn't have time to argue. She walked toward the ladies' room, hoping the ridiculous cat mask would hide her identity. Vince and Dave didn't even glance at her as she entered and paused behind the door. She kept it slightly ajar so she could watch and listen.

"No, it was a witch," the boy said adamantly.

"A *real* witch?" Dave asked.

Vince jabbed Dave hard with his elbow. Then he turned to the boy and said with a forced smile, "There's no such thing as witches, son. What's your name?"

"Bobby Barnswell."

"And how old are you, Bobby?"

"Eleven." Bobby folded his arms across his chest and looked Vince in the eye. "I know what I saw, mister, and it was a witch."

Annie bit her lip to keep from gasping. Vince's next question was the same one that was on her mind.

"What, exactly, did you see?"

"Her eyes were glowing, and she made a bunch of trash cans chase me. Then she blew up a padlock with her bare hands. If you don't believe me, go out there and look for yourself."

"I'll do that." Vince hesitated. "Can you describe her?"

"Sure. She looked like a witch."

"Could you be a little more specific?" Vince asked tightly.

Annie recognized the edge in Vince's voice. He was frustrated and losing patience, but like her, he was anxious to hear what Bobby had to say.

Bobby rolled his eyes. "She had warts and a big nose and cracked skin and clumps of gray hair on a bald head."

"Yeah," Dave said. "She looked like a witch."

"Right." Vince shook his head and sighed. "Look, kid. It's been nice talking to you, but—"

Annie held her breath. Bobby's story sounded preposterous. Vince might think the kid was over-reacting to monster movies and Halloween and let it drop.

"And she was wearing jeans and a striped T-shirt with long sleeves," Bobby added thoughtfully.

Vince's interest increased suddenly. "Jeans and a T-shirt?"

"Yep. I'm sure of it." Bobby nodded.

"Don't go away, kid. We'll be right back." Motioning for Dave to follow, Vince hurried toward the emergency exit.

Annie let the rest room door close and sagged

against it to collect her thoughts. Although Bobby Barnswell couldn't positively identify Alex, he had gotten a pretty close look at her. Close enough to see her do some really strange things.

Even worse, Annie realized, Vince believed Bobby.

CHAPTER 5

Alex watched the theater while she waited for the golden glow to fade. Several minutes passed and no one came out to search the alley. Could she be safe? Maybe the boy hadn't told anyone what he had seen because he knew his story was too outrageous to be believed. Adults had a tendency to ignore such things . . . unless there was evidence.

But then Alex wondered. Was there something in the alley that would support the boy's story?

She frowned. The folded witch mask was in her back pocket. No problem. Anyone could have toppled and rolled a bunch of trash cans, and the wire gate had cooled down by now. But, she realized anxiously, the broken padlock might provide a clue. It hadn't been forced and broken with a hammer or anything. It had been demolished with a super powerful electrical charge.

Alex realized she couldn't leave the padlock behind. If the plant lab technicians ever asked about it, Bobby could say that he'd seen her take off down the alley, and the plant people could figure the rest out. Then Danielle Atron would know that a young girl had zapped it with her bare hands.

Alex darted across the street to the back of the theater. She crept to the corner of the building and peeked into the alley. The coast was clear. Dashing to the gate, she picked up both pieces of the broken padlock.

At the same moment the emergency door opened.

"How do you *know* there's no such thing as a real witch, Vince?" Dave's voice echoed in the short hallway.

Alex didn't have time to run, and there was nowhere to hide—at least not as a girl. Still gripping the padlock, she morphed into a puddle again.

"I just know, Dave!" Vince entered the alley just as Alex slid behind some empty cardboard boxes stacked by the fence. He had taken off his helmet and was still carrying the GC 161 detector.

Alex trembled with fright as Vince's icy blue eyes scanned the alley. He had not seen her ooze into hiding, but she had to be careful making her getaway. A sudden move might disturb the boxes and alert the security man to her presence.

Dave came out behind Vince, scratching his bald, plastic head. "Maybe witches only come out on Halloween, like vampires and ghosts. And zombies and trolls. . . ."

"Enough already!" Vince spat out. "There are no vampires, Dave. No ghosts and no witches!" With a frustrated sigh, Vince turned his attention to the detector, which was flashing a green light.

"Then how do you explain what Bobby saw?" Dave blathered on. "Glowing eyes and flying trash cans. Kinda strange, don't you think?"

"Very strange." Vince walked up to one of the trash cans lying in the middle of the alley and kicked it. The can rolled, spilling more papers on the pavement. "That's what's so intriguing. We don't know what that massive dosage of GC 161 did to the kid. The side effects may be more extraordinary than we thought."

Chills rippled through Alex's liquid self. The

boy's report about a glowing witch who made trash cans fly would seem like Halloween hysteria to everyone but Vince. He *knew* GC 161 was a powerful compound with unknown effects, and he *wanted* to find something really weird.

Alex just wanted to get away. She didn't know how close Vince had to be before the device detected GC 161 and started blinking red, and she didn't want to find out.

When Vince started toward the gate, Alex saw her chance. She elongated herself and cautiously slid through the boxes to the theater wall. Using a cement gutter for cover, she oozed into a drainpipe.

"Can I go back inside?" Dave asked.

"Yeah, sure." Eyes on the detector, Vince waved absently.

"I've got to find my nose. . . ." Dave muttered as he stepped back through the emergency door.

Huddling in the damp metal tube, Alex watched as Vince studied the wire gate and the ground around it. He was roughly twenty feet from her position, and the light stayed green.

Finding nothing, Vince left after an agonizing couple of minutes. Alex waited a minute more, then slithered out of the pipe. She didn't change back into herself until she was three buildings away.

Stuffing the padlock into her pocket with the witch mask, Alex started home. Even though Vince hadn't found anything to prove Bobby was telling the truth, he had been willing to spend a long time searching for her, following up on any lead that might help track her down.

And he was getting closer, Alex thought desperately. Which meant she had a majorly big problem. There was no doubt that Vince would have his new GC 161 detectors set up at the plant party that night.

Alex turned the corner down her street. Somehow, she had to convince her parents to let her stay home. She just had to!

"Alex?" Mrs. Mack pulled up to the curb in the family car.

Alex looked up, startled for a moment. "Oh, it's you. Hi, Mom!"

"The movie's not over already, is it?" Mrs. Mack asked.

"Uh, no. I, uh—" Alex hesitated. Her mom knew how much she had been looking forward to the Monster Movie Matinee. The only logical reason Alex would leave early would be illness. And if her mother believed her, that would be the perfect excuse to get out of the party tonight!

Holding her stomach, Alex made a face. "I'm not feeling very well, Mom."

"Too much popcorn and candy?" Mrs. Mack asked with a sympathetic smile.

"I don't think so. I didn't feel great when I got up this morning." Alex winced, hoping her act was convincing. Her mom wouldn't let her off the hook for stuffing herself with sweets.

"Well, get in. I'll take you home after I pick up some more candy for the trick-or-treaters tonight." Mrs. Mack gestured toward the passenger door.

At least not all of my luck is bad, Alex thought as she slid into the front seat and closed the car door. Now she had the perfect out for the party.

"Then I'll call the clinic and see if I can get you in for a checkup this afternoon."

"Checkup?"

Mrs. Mack nodded thoughtfully. "Maybe it's nothing serious, Alex. I know you don't want to miss the party tonight, but it wouldn't be right to go if you've got something contagious."

"I'm not contagious," Alex said quickly. She just *couldn't* have a medical examination. A doctor would discover that there was an unnatural chemical in her system. For all she knew, Danielle Atron had asked all the doctors in town to report any strange medical problems they found in the local teenagers.

So much for that brilliant idea, Alex thought. Now she had to convince her mother that she was really okay. Maybe Annie could think of a good reason she should stay home that night. And if that failed, her sister, the brain, could just put that I.Q. to good use and figure out a way to avoid the detectors at the party.

Where is Annie, anyway? Alex sighed, wondering. When she got into trouble, Annie was the one person she could count on to get her out of it.

"Do you want to wait in the car?" Mrs. Mack asked as she pulled into the discount store parking lot.

"No. Actually, I'm feeling a lot better now." Alex smiled and shrugged. "It must have been something I ate after all."

"Well, if you're sure. . . ."

"I'm sure." Alex bounced out of the car and jogged ahead of her mom as proof positive that she was in perfect health.

Barbara Mack did not take time to browse through the store's sale racks as usual. She went directly to the Halloween candy display, selected a half-dozen bags of popular treats, and zipped through the express checkout. Alex wasn't surprised. Her mom was dressing as a Japanese Geisha for the party and she needed plenty of time to apply the heavy makeup. Her father was going as a Samurai warrior.

"Did you get all the beaded necklaces you wanted for your gypsy costume?" Mrs. Mack asked as they started to exit.

"Yeah. Nicole's mother gave me three she doesn't wear anymore, and Robyn loaned me a bangled bracelet. I'm all set."

Alex trailed behind her mother across the parking lot. Unlike Annie, Alex had been eagerly anticipating the party. She couldn't wait to dress up in the full, colorful skirt and white peasant blouse and wear lots of jangling beads and bangles. And Robyn was coming over later to do her makeup.

"Alex!" Mrs. Mack snapped. "Watch where you're going!"

Alex stopped short as a car pulled into the parking space right in front of her. The next scared her, but not as much as the shock of seeing the boy in the front seat.

Bobby!

Heart hammering and pulse racing, Alex didn't even have to look at her hands to know she was starting to glow again. She whipped the old witch mask out of her pocket, then heard a clunk as something fell on the pavement. Slipping on the mask, she looked down and saw the broken padlock.

"I'm not making it up, Mom," Bobby said as he opened his car door. "I saw a real witch at the movie, I swear."

Stooping, Alex grabbed the padlock with her golden hand and ducked behind the pickup truck parked next to Bobby's car. Shoving the lock back into her pocket, she pulled her hands up into her long sleeves.

"There's no such thing as witches, Bobby." The boy's mother grinned.

"That Vince guy from the plant believes me," Bobby said.

Alex moved to the front of the truck as Bobby and his mother passed by.

"And I'm gonna help him find her," Bobby said atically. "She's worse than Frankenstein's Mom, 'cause she can do magic stuff. I

Bobby's mother shook her head. "Maybe you've been watching too many monster movies."

"Alex?" Mrs. Mack called and looked around the parking lot with a puzzled expression. "Alex!"

Still squatting, Alex edged around to the far side of the truck. She didn't dare answer her mother or show herself until Bobby was farther away.

"This isn't a movie, Mom," Bobby insisted stubbornly. "This is real life."

"Alex! Where are you?"

How do I explain this? Alex wondered. Not only was she glowing like a jack-o'-lantern, she was hiding from her mother like a mischievous little kid. *Which gave her another bright idea. . . .*

Creeping to the back of Bobby's car, Alex waited another few seconds. Then, hiding her hands in the front pockets of her jeans, she sprang up with a blood-curdling shriek. "Gotcha!"

Startled, Mrs. Mack dropped her bag. Her hand flew to her chest to still her pounding heart. "Alexandra Mack! What do you think you're doing?"

"Just getting into the Halloween mood," Alex explained, laughing. "Sorry."

Mrs. Mack frowned and shook her head. She unlocked the car and got in. Alex opened the passenger door, noticing that the dimmer but had not quite disappeared. She kept her hands in her pockets as she slid into the front seat.

"Well, I guess you are feeling better." Mrs. Mack turned to say something else and just stared.

"What?" Alex knew her mom saw the glow around the edge of her mask, but she was ready with an explanation this time.

"Why are you glowing?"

"Neat, huh? It's the latest thing. Glow-stick Halloween masks. They look really creepy in the dark, but they're easy to see, too. So kids are safer while they're out trick-or-treating."

Mrs. Mack nodded, impressed. "Not a bad idea, actually. Somebody's going to make a fortune selling those. But no more 'gotchas,' okay? I'm much too young to have a heart attack."

"Okay." Alex relaxed but decided not to risk taking the mask off just yet. If her mom saw her younger daughter's *whole* face shining like the full moon, that was a Halloween trick Alex couldn't possibly explain.

CHAPTER 6

Annie was munching on celery sticks and pacing in the kitchen when Alex and Mrs. Mack arrived home.

"Hi, Annie." Mrs. Mack dropped the bag of candy on the kitchen counter and immediately went to check the answering machine in the living room.

"Where have you been, Alex? I've been worried sick." Annie spoke in rapid hushed tones.

"Trying not to get caught, that's where. Where have you been?" Alex took off the witch mask and breathed in deeply.

"Gathering information. Come on." Annie tugged on Alex's sleeve. "We can't talk here."

Alex followed Annie into the garage and sank onto an overturned milk crate. She was exhausted from making too many narrow escapes. Thankfully, she and Annie had a place to go to get away from their mother. Annie used the garage as a lab for her chemistry experiments, so Mrs. Mack wouldn't wonder why they were out here.

"We've got a problem," Annie said.

"We've got two problems," Alex replied. "Vince's new detector and Bobby." She dropped her chin onto her hands and sighed.

"So what happened?" Annie asked. "Exactly?"

Alex told Annie everything, starting with her flight from the theater and ending with the glow-stick explanation to their mom.

"And she believed you?" Annie laughed.

"A mask that lights up is a lot easier to believe than a face that lights up."

"Guess you're right about that." Annie smiled and patted Alex on the shoulder. "You really handled yourself well, Alex."

"Think so?" Alex asked, surprised by the unexpected praise. Most of the time she had to explain to Annie why she had done something stupid.

"Definitely," Annie said. "Making sure Vince didn't find that padlock was absolutely the right thing to do. And Bobby Barnswell really thinks he saw a witch, not a girl with inexplicable powers."

"But Vince knows something weird happened at the theater."

"All he's got is a kid's word, and he can't prove anything." Annie held out her hand. "Give me that padlock, and I'll get rid of it—after I run my own tests."

Alex handed Annie the fried lock. "He won't need Bobby as a witness tonight, Annie. The GC 161 detectors will find me."

"Not if you don't go." Annie stashed the padlock in a shoebox and stowed it under the train table.

"There's no way to get out of it, Annie," Alex said glumly. "I used being sick as an excuse for leaving the movie early, and Mom wanted to take me right to the clinic. So then I had to say I wasn't sick anymore."

"My plan is a bit more complex than that." Annie grinned as she pulled up a piano stool and sat down. "I think I've figured out how you can go to the party and *not* be there."

"Huh?" Alex said. "What are you going to do, clone me?"

"Just listen! There's more to this problem than just making sure you don't get near those new detectors. Danielle Atron *is* setting a trap, and she's made it clear to everyone's parents that their kids are expected to come to the party, too."

"That much is certain," Alex mumbled glumly.

"She'll suspect any kid who *isn't* there, especially if the detectors *don't* find GC 161 in the kids who do attend. So you've got to go."

"Right." Alex wondered if Annie was finally losing it.

"Have you got any money?" Annie asked.

"Twelve dollars and some change I've been saving for a new pair of roller blades. Why?"

"And I've got twenty. That ought to be enough." Annie frowned as she did some quick calculations in her head.

"Enough for what?" Alex asked.

"Two identical witch costumes. Marvin's Costume Shop has loads. Guess they're not very popular this year."

"Witch costumes! *I'm* not wearing a witch costume, Annie. If I'm going at all tonight, I'm going as a gypsy."

"Fine. Get caught."

Alex surrendered—reluctantly. "Okay. What's the plan?"

"We dress alike and both go to the party. Then you leave and I'll sneak out without telling anybody and come back as you."

"Uh-huh. And where will I be?" Alex asked, trying to visualize how this twin-witch scenario might work.

"Hiding in the car. It's a master plan."

"Except for a couple of things." Alex was not used to finding holes in Annie's schemes, but these were too obvious to ignore. "Bobby's looking for a witch."

"And Vince is looking for a scared kid who *knows* Bobby thinks he saw a witch. Anyone dressed like a witch will be less suspicious."

"Maybe." That argument did make sense, Alex decided. "But how are you going to sneak out without being seen? Vince will have guards everywhere, especially at the exits and entrances."

"Your powers of reasoning are improving, Alex." Annie sighed. "Unfortunately, that's the one part of the plan I haven't figured out yet. But I will."

"Hey!" Raymond shouted and banged on the side door. "Are you guys in there?"

"Yes, Ray." Annie rose with a pained sigh and went to unlock the door. "Come on in."

Ray swept into the garage wearing a long black cape lined in red. He held an edge of the cape over the lower half of his face. "I am Count Dracula," he said, imitating Bela Lugosi's deep voice.

"Cool cape, Ray!" Alex exclaimed. "You didn't tell me you were dressing up as a vampire."

"Not just a vampire. Count Dracula!" Raymond narrowed his eyes and slowly advanced toward Alex. "I want to—"

"Yes!" Annie jumped in front of him, stopping him with an outstretched hand. "Let me see this."

"You like it?" Ray asked in his own voice.

"This is what you're wearing to the party tonight, right?" Annie asked.

"It's part of my costume. But it's too long. See?" Ray threw his arms out with a flourish and turned to demonstrate that the cape dragged on the floor.

"No, it's not. It's perfect." Annie nodded with approval.

"It is?" Ray's eyes went wide as Annie suddenly ducked underneath the long cape. "What—"

"Just hold still a minute, Ray," Annie said.

Alex instantly clued in to Annie's idea and jumped up to inspect the effect. Annie could hide under the cape. It just might work. "Draw it closed in front," Alex said.

"Is this some kind of weird joke?" Ray asked.

"No, honest. Just cooperate for a minute, please?" Annie said.

Ray hesitated, then drew the cape closed.

"Can you see me?" Annie asked.

Alex stood back. "It's all bumpy in back, Annie. Pretty obvious that someone's under there." She paused thoughtfully. "Swoop across the floor, Ray."

"Swoop? What's swoop?"

"You know. Swoop." Alex waved her arms. "Walk fast so the cape kinda billows out in back."

"Oh! Swoop!" Raymond glided across the floor with Annie trying to match his stride. He turned and glided back, but it was still obvious that someone was hiding underneath. "How's that?"

"I don't think it's going to work, but it was worth a try." Alex's shoulders sagged.

Annie crawled out from under the cape and rubbed her shin. "You have bony legs, Raymond."

"I didn't expect to be sharing my costume, Annie." Confused, Raymond looked back and forth from Annie to Alex. "Will someone please explain to me *why* I'm sharing my costume?"

Alex quickly explained the problem and the plan. Once he understood, Raymond pitched in with some ideas of his own.

"If I keep my back to a wall, it might work." Raymond motioned for Annie to get under the cape again.

After they practiced moving for a few minutes, Alex felt a rush of new hope. Looking at Raymond head on, no one could tell another person was under the cape.

"Don't worry about getting there ahead of me," Raymond said. "My Dad's on the refreshment committee, so I'll be there early."

"Thanks for helping us out, Ray," Alex said sincerely.

"No problem, Alex. It's just too bad you're going to miss all the fun. There's going to be dancing and door prizes and a costume contest. First prize is fifty dollars."

"Yeah, well. Better to miss the party than to miss the rest of my life 'cause Danielle Atron found out who I am."

"That's the truth. See ya later, guys."

When Raymond was gone, Annie focused on the other, necessary details. "Costumes first."

"Right. I'll go get my money." Alex paused on her way into the kitchen. "Listen, Annie. I know you don't want to go to this party. You could have gotten out of it somehow, and now you have to show up as a geeky witch just to help me—again."

"Don't worry about it. The only way I could get rid of Jason to look for you at the theater was to promise I'd be there tonight." Annie rolled her eyes and sighed with weary resignation.

"I'm not blind, Annie Mack. You like him."

"I don't know whether I do or not." Annie shrugged, then smiled slightly. "The only way to find out is to get to know him better, right?"

"Right."

"Besides, if Jason turns out to be a dork, our little plan provides *me* with the perfect escape." Annie's dark eyes twinkled.

"Like how?" Alex asked.

"Like if I can't stand him, I'll just pretend to be you."

CHAPTER 7

"Company, Alex!" Mrs. Mack yelled from downstairs. "It's Robyn and Nicole."

"Send them up," Alex shouted back. She had been lying in bed, staring at the ceiling since Annie had left for Marvin's Costume Shop over an hour ago. What was taking her so long? Maybe Marvin's had run out of witch costumes at the last minute.

Sitting up, Alex gazed wistfully at the gypsy costume arranged on the end of her bed. She and her sister needed two identical outfits for the plan to work, but Alex hated having to go to the party as a witch. Even though she wouldn't actually *be* there, everyone would *think* she was there—dressed in a childish costume and wearing a dorky mask. With luck, she might live it down by the ninth grade.

"Hey, Alex!" Nicole bounded into the room. "So tell me. When did you become a magician?"

"Huh?" Alex blinked.

"That was the coolest disappearing act I've ever seen."

"Totally," Robyn agreed. She slipped a backpack off her shoulder and dropped it on the floor.

Alex stared at her friends in horror. Had they seen her morph her way out of the movie today?

Nicole grinned as she perched on the edge of Annie's bed. "One minute you were there, then presto! I turn around and you're gone. Pretty slick."

Relieved, Alex exhaled slowly. They hadn't seen her use her powers after all. "I, uh—wasn't feeling well, so I just—slipped out quietly."

"You do look kind of pale," Robyn said.

No wonder, Alex thought dismally. Worrying about Robyn and Nicole finding out about her powers was enough to make her look sick. And she hated not being able to tell them. They told each other everything. Like Raymond, they were her *best* friends, and she knew they wouldn't do

69

or say anything that would endanger her. But Annie was adamant about keeping it a secret. That way the people at the plant would never go after Nicole or Robyn.

"I'm fine now," Alex said. "Just something I ate, I guess."

"Well, I can certainly sympathize with that." Robyn sighed. "I have a violent reaction if I even *smell* a banana." Robyn was a pale redhead, and very sensitive.

"Pesticides are the real problem." Nicole's eyes flashed. "I'd rather share a tomato with a bug than be poisoned. How much can a bug eat anyway?"

"Swarming locusts can wipe out an entire crop in seconds," Robyn countered. Sometimes she and Alex liked to get Nicole riled up about whatever current cause she was into.

"Nature's revenge against pesticides," Nicole shot back. "Locust riots."

"Speaking of riots . . ." Robyn turned back to Alex. "Too bad you didn't wait an extra five minutes before you left the movie."

"Yeah. Those dweeb ushers almost started a riot in the theater." Crossing her arms, Nicole shook her head. "What was their problem anyway?"

"Beats me." Robyn sighed.

"Haven't got a clue," Alex added, relieved that her friends thought that Vince and Dave were only ushers. Then she quickly changed the subject. "What's in the bag, Robyn?"

"*You* are gonna love this!" Vince and Dave's disruptive antics in the theater were forgotten as Robyn opened her backpack. "I found some really cool accessories for your gypsy costume." She pulled out a long, red silk scarf. "For your hair."

"Nice." Alex nodded and smiled tightly. *Uh-oh,* she thought. *How am I going to explain this one?*

"And these!" Robyn held out a pair of gigantic, gold hoop earrings.

"They're great, Robyn. They really are, but—"

"But?" Nicole scowled. "Don't you like them, Alex?"

"No, I think they're super! It's just that—" Alex tried to act unconcerned and casual. "I've, uh—changed my mind about my costume, that's all."

"You're not going to wear your gypsy outfit?" Robyn's mouth fell open. "But why not? You look absolutely gorgeous in that costume."

"Too true. No way Scott could ignore you in that getup." Nicole stood and picked up the red, green, gold, and white skirt lying on Alex's bed. She held

71

it to her waist and twirled to check the flair effect. "I think you're making a big mistake."

"I have my reasons," Alex said.

"So what are you going to wear?" Nicole asked.

"Something cool, I bet." Robyn nodded knowingly. "It's guaranteed Kelly will look totally perfect."

"Something—different." Alex shrugged. "Sort of."

"What do you mean, 'sort of'?" Nicole asked.

Before the girls could press the issue, Annie burst through the door. "What a mob scene!"

Alex held her breath as Annie stopped abruptly with her mouth hanging open. She hadn't expected Robyn and Nicole to be there, but luckily she caught herself before she said anything about tonight's plan.

"Hi, Robyn. Nicole," Annie said after an awkward moment's hesitation. She grinned at Alex. "Sorry I took so long. Half the town's at the costume shop this afternoon."

"What did you get?" Robyn asked curiously.

"Alex's costume. Want to see?" As Annie reached into the huge plastic bag, Robyn and Nicole leaned in for a closer look.

Behind their backs, Alex shook her head and

waved her hands at Annie. Trying to explain why she had decided to dress up as a stupid witch instead of a beautiful gypsy dancer would be hard enough after the party. But by then the damage to her social standing would be done. She didn't want to try now because she knew Robyn and Nicole would try to talk her out of it.

Annie ignored her and pulled out a black, pointed witch's hat. She handed it to a stunned Robyn, then gave an ugly, flexible plastic, full-head witch mask to a speechless Nicole. "Cool, huh?" Annie said. "No one will guess who she is in a million years."

Alex groaned. The realistic mask sported a hooked nose, hairy warts, dark wrinkles, and long tangles of coarse black hair. It was hideous beyond belief. "Cool" was definitely not the word for it.

"Well." Holding the witch hat by the point, Robyn dangled it in front of her. "It's certainly . . . Halloweeny."

"You're going to the party as an old hag?" Nicole asked Alex incredulously. "Was this your idea?"

"Of course." Alex jumped up and took the mask from Nicole's hand. "We can dress up in pretty stuff anytime, but Halloween is the only night of the year we can be spooky and . . . and weird. That's the fun!"

"Exactly." Annie stuffed the hat back in the bag and avoided looking Alex in the eye. "Raymond's going as Count Dracula. They'll be the perfect couple."

"More like the Odd Couple." Nicole's frown deepened as she glanced at Robyn and said, "Maybe she really is sick."

"And delirious with fever." Robyn placed her hand on Alex's forehead. "Nope. She's cool."

"That's a debatable observation," Nicole muttered.

"There's nothing wrong with me," Alex protested. She was desperate to salvage some of her damaged dignity, but she couldn't think of any reasoning that made sense. Her sister came to the rescue.

"Real cool," Annie said, "is having the self-confidence to dress up as something ugly and bizarre because it's fun."

"Yeah!" Robyn nodded. "That's true, isn't it?"

"I hadn't thought about it that way," Nicole said sheepishly. "Kelly wouldn't have the guts, that's for sure. Sorry, Alex."

"That's okay, Nicole," Alex said honestly. Her

friends hadn't meant their comments to be mean. They had been understandably bewildered by Alex's decision to wear the witch costume.

"Well, guess you won't need me for makeup." Robyn stuffed the scarf back into her bag.

"I gotta get going anyway." Nicole threw up her hands. "I don't have a clue what I'm going to be tonight."

"I thought you were going as toxic waste," Robyn said.

"Great idea, but I haven't had time to make a costume. Too much homework lately. So I'm stuck."

"I know it's not your usual style, Nicole," Alex said, "but you can wear my gypsy costume if you want."

A sparkle dawned in Nicole's dark eyes. "I guess someone should wear it, huh? You worked so hard to put it all together." She picked up the skirt and blouse, then glanced at Alex. "You're sure about this?"

"Absolutely. Take it. You'll look great." Alex smiled as the girls gathered up the accessories. She turned on Annie like a sudden, summer thunderstorm the moment they were gone. "How could you humiliate me like that, Annie?"

"Strategy," Annie said calmly.

"I mean, it's bad enough I'm gonna miss the party entirely and that everyone will think I showed up in that—that awful witch thing, but you didn't have to make me look like a complete fool in front of my best friends!"

"I wasn't trying to embarrass you, Alex. Honest."

"Since when?" Fuming, Alex crossed her arms and glared.

"It's like this," Annie said patiently. "You wouldn't ignore Robyn and Nicole if you were at the party, right? You'd hang out with them."

"Yeah. So?"

"So *I'm* going to have to spend time with them pretending to be *you*. Not an easy thing to pull off, Alex. They're your best friends. Showing them your witch costume will support the illusion. They'll *assume* I'm you and that you're just acting a little strange because it's Halloween."

"How strange?" Alex asked.

"I'll have to disguise my voice to fool them, Alex. Might as well play the witch to the max. Some grunting and cackling—"

"You're going to cackle?" Alex was appalled. Everyone would think she was a total dweeb.

"Trust me, Alex. It's the only way."

Groaning, Alex flopped down on her bed. As usual, Annie was right. She had to do whatever was necessary to throw Vince and Danielle Atron off her trail.

Annie paused in the doorway on her way to the bathroom. "That was a really nice thing you did for Nicole, Alex. I know how much you wanted to wear the gypsy outfit."

Alex just shrugged. Helping out Nicole did make her feel better, but not much. After the party, her cool-quotient would be zero.

"Alex?" Mrs. Mack's voice drifted down the hall. "Alex!"

"Coming!" Alex dragged herself to her mother's room. Mrs. Mack poked her head out of the master bathroom. Her face was covered with white powder. In spite of her depressed mood, Alex had to bite her lip to keep from giggling.

"Where's Annie?" Mrs. Mack asked.

"Taking a shower."

Mr. Mack walked in carrying his Samurai costume. "I think I'm going to need some help with this, Barbara."

"Just a minute, George." Mrs. Mack looked at Alex. "Putting on this makeup is going to take longer than I thought. Will you answer the door for the trick-or-treaters, Alex? Annie can take over after she's dressed so you can get ready."

"No problem." Actually, Alex had been looking forward to handing out treats rather than going door-to-door herself. Besides, it wouldn't take more than five minutes to get into the witch costume.

"The candy's already in a bowl by the front door." Mrs. Mack smiled and ducked back into the bathroom. "Thanks."

The doorbell rang as Alex started down the stairs. Anxious to answer before the neighborhood goblins got impatient and decided to play a mischievous trick, Alex threw open the door.

A father with two small children stood on the front porch. The little girl wore a bunny costume and the boy wore a clear plastic bag stuffed with colored balloons.

"Trick-or-treat!"

"What are you supposed to be?" Alex asked the boy as she dropped candy bars into their plastic pumpkins.

"A bag of jelly beans!" The little boy sighed dramatically and rolled his eyes as though that should be obvious.

Alex chuckled as they left and three boys dressed in different colored Rocket Ranger jumpsuits jogged up to take their place. Two wore white helmet masks and the boy in the middle wore black, with an orange lightning bolt down the front of his jumpsuit.

"Trick-or-treat," the black-masked boy said. "We're in a hurry and we need supplies."

"Yeah," the other two boys agreed.

"Don't you guys look cool." As Alex reached into the candy bowl, the middle boy raised his mask to see the selection more clearly.

Bobby Barnswell!

Stunned, Alex froze and the boys helped themselves to chocolate bars.

"Thanks." Bobby looked up with a somber expression.

"You guys have a good time, okay?" Alex struggled to stay calm as she met the boy's stare. If she started to glow now, it would be all over.

"We're on a mission tonight," Bobby said seriously. "But don't worry. The Rocket Rangers always catch the bad guy."

"Yeah!" The boy on the left nodded. "Even if the bad guy's a real witch."

As Bobby led his troops back down the walk, he turned and looked back.

Alex quickly closed the door and sagged against it. She didn't think Bobby had recognized her, but he was as determined to catch the witch as Vince was to find the GC 161 kid.

They were a dangerous combination.

CHAPTER 8

"Okay, I give up," Mrs. Mack said. "Which witch is which?"

Alex grinned under the ugly mask and glanced down at Annie. Their black dresses had fringed hems that drooped over the tops of their matching black running shoes. Potion pouches hung from rope belts, and short, fringed capes were attached to the high collars. Wearing wide-brimmed, pointed hats and holding witch's brooms, they had paused on different stairs for inspection. Annie was a little taller than Alex, the only difference that might give their parents a clue.

"Twin witches? What a great idea!" Mr. Mack exclaimed. Dressed in formal Samurai brocades, their father looked elegantly dignified.

Neither Alex nor Annie said a word.

"I thought you were going as a gypsy, Alex." Mrs. Mack shifted her gaze between the two girls. "Alex?" She looked at Annie. "Annie?" She looked at Alex.

"Wrong!" Annie raised her hand for a victorious high-five.

"Yes!" Slapping Annie's palm, Alex burst out laughing. If their mother and father couldn't tell them apart, they could fool everyone else, too.

"Okay, gang," Mr. Mack said. "We'd better get going."

"Heh, heh, heh . . ." Annie cackled in a gravelly voice. She hunched over slightly and waved a crooked finger at Mr. Mack. "I've got a new spell I can't wait to try. Heh, heh, heh . . ."

Annie was throwing herself into the part with surprising enthusiasm. *But then*, Alex thought, *Annie doesn't have to worry about her reputation. Everyone at the party will think she's me—the weird witch!*

"Better beware," Alex cackled in a similar voice. "We're very fond of toads. Heh, heh, heh."

"Double, double, toil and trouble. . . ." Mr. Mack grinned, then sighed when the girls didn't comment. "*Macbeth*. Shakespeare?"

"Fire burn . . ." Annie recited in her witch's voice.

". . . and cauldron bubble." Alex finished the line.

"I'm impressed." Tucking her hands into the wide sleeves of her blue and white kimono, Mrs. Mack stepped back to let the girls through the doorway. "If you two can stay in character all night, you'll be the hit of the party."

"You might even win something," Mr. Mack said. "The prize for best costume is fifty dollars."

"Ah-hah!" Annie nodded. "More than enough to stock up on frogs' eyes and lizard innards."

"Pigs' feet and owl feathers," Alex added as she shuffled behind Annie to the car.

When they arrived at the plant, the parking lot was almost full. Mr. Mack finally gave up trying to find a space close to the administration building and parked by the factory complex. As the family headed across the wide lot, Alex and Annie lagged behind. They didn't want their parents to notice that Alex had left her broom in the car.

"You remember what to do, right?" Annie whispered.

"Yeah." Alex took a deep breath to soothe her jangled nerves. "What if they have detectors out here?"

"They won't," Annie said confidently. "They can't scan everyone individually out here."

Mr. and Mrs. Mack entered the building through double glass doors and paused to chat with a cowboy and a woman dressed as a frontier settler. Alex and Annie waited anxiously, then followed the adults to the party entrance on the far side of the lobby.

The entrance to the room was decorated like the front of a haunted house. Eerie howls, moans, and shrieks came from speakers above the doorway. A ghost and a zombie were stationed in front of the room with a guest book. They took the names of everyone who entered, and stamped their hands. Beyond the entrance was a narrow hallway.

"Clever," Annie whispered. "The detectors must be inside that corridor. Everyone has to enter single file, and the guards are taking names. If the device is triggered, they'll know who did it." She hesitated. "You have to get ID'd and stamped *before* you remember you forgot your broom, okay?"

"Got it."

"You'll be fine," Annie said reassuringly. "Come on."

Alex's stomach churned and her mouth went dry when they stopped by the entrance.

Annie raised her mask. "Annie Mack."

The zombie-guard noted her name, then stamped her hand with an invisible marker that showed up under a special flashlight.

Taking a big breath, Alex stepped up and lifted her own mask. "Alex Mack." She quickly covered her face again.

The guard started slightly when he realized Alex was dressed exactly like Annie. "Twins?"

"Like two peas in a pod," Annie said, jumping on the unexpected opportunity. "Can't tell us apart, can you?"

"Yes, I can." The zombie guard stamped Alex's hand and grinned. "She's got a broom, and you don't."

Alex stifled a surprised squeal of delight. *How totally perfect!* If the rest of Annie's plan went this smoothly, they didn't have anything to worry about.

"Gosh, Annie! I left it in the car!" Alex wailed. She was glad the mask covered the big grin on her face. As she ran toward the glass doors, she shouted to Annie, "Don't you dare do anything cool before I get back!"

Alex ran outside and dashed across the parking lot to the car. All she had to do now was hide and wait.

The rest was up to Annie and Raymond.

As Annie stepped out of the passageway, she spotted Vince, Dave, and three boys dressed as Rocket Rangers standing by a panel of high-tech electronic equipment. *Bobby Barnswell and friends, no doubt.* Dave was still wearing his clown costume, but Vince had changed into a suit and tie. She did not look at them as she hurried toward Raymond, who was by the refreshment table munching on a cinnamon-apple doughnut.

"Annie!" Dusting sugar off his hands, Raymond executed a sweeping bow. He was wearing a tux under the long, black cape. A bright red half-mask over his eyes matched the red lining. He popped fake vampire teeth into his mouth and said, "Dracula at your service."

"Very effective, Raymond. Now let's go. I have to get out and back in before too long or the guards might get suspicious."

"That's gonna be tricky." Raymond's speech was slightly garbled by the false fangs. "The only way in or out is the main entrance. If we use an emergency exit, we'll set off the alarms."

Annie's brain stalled for a brief second. It had been foolish to think they could sneak by Vince when he was waiting for something weird to happen. And even if they got into the lobby safely, leaving through the glass doors was too risky. The costumed guards might notice the extra humps under Raymond's cape.

"There's got to be a way!" Annie insisted.

"There is," Raymond said. "You'll just have to trust me." Annie hesitated, then nodded. She didn't have a plan B. Slipping under the cape, she did her best to match Raymond's movements when he began to move slowly along the wall.

"I'm gonna walk a little faster," Raymond whispered. "Nobody's coming in now, and Vince isn't paying much attention."

Raymond had a point there, Annie realized. Anyone leaving the party had already been scanned and cleared.

"Right after I talk to the guards," Raymond continued, "we're going to make a hard right turn."

"Okay." Annie desperately tried not to stumble over Raymond's feet as he broke into a fast walk.

"Hey, Count!" One of the guards spoke. "What's the hurry?"

"Too much cider!" Raymond answered.

Annie braced herself and scurried sideways as Raymond turned right. A moment later, they went through two doors and stopped.

"Okay, Annie. We're here."

"Where's here?" Annie stepped out from under the cape, straightened, then gasped. "The men's room? Raymond!"

Crossing his arms, Raymond eyed her indignantly. "Don't you think someone might have noticed Count Dracula going into the ladies' room?"

"You're probably right," Annie sighed.

"Besides, I didn't know if there was a window in the ladies' room. Come on. I'll give you a boost."

Annie didn't need to be coaxed. She wanted out before someone else came in. Stepping into Raymond's cupped hands, she unlatched the high window and pushed it open. The area below it was shielded by a tall row of hedges. Tossing her broom outside, she balanced herself on the sill, drew her legs through the opening, then dropped to the ground feet-first. Picking up the broom,

Annie darted between cars into the parking lot, then ran back toward the glass doors.

"Well," the zombie guard said as Annie slid to a breathless halt by the entrance. "Now that you've got your broom, I'll never be able to tell you or your sister apart."

Annie just nodded as the guard checked her stamped hand with the flashlight, then waved her on.

As she entered the main room, neither Vince nor Bobby Barnswell gave her a second glance. However, Robyn and Nicole had been waiting for Alex to arrive.

"Yo, Alex!" Nicole twirled to show off the gypsy costume. "What do you think?"

Wearing a pink poodle skirt, a white blouse with puffed sleeves, saddle shoes, and white socks, Robyn tugged on her ponytail. "I think she looks keen."

"Keen?" Nicole asked, bewildered.

"That's fifties talk for cool," Robyn explained. "Tell her she looks great, Alex, or she'll worry about it all night."

Annie immediately shifted into witch mode— Alex style. Hunching over, she waggled a finger at

Nicole. "Too pretty. Maybe I should turn you into a toad. Heh, heh, heh."

"Neat-o, but don't you mean frog?" Robyn asked.

"No, I mean toad. I turn princes into frogs." Annie sighed. Suddenly, getting past Vince and the guards seemed easy compared to pretending to be Alex pretending to be a witch.

"Alex?" Looking like a major hunk in black, silver-studded leather, Jason smiled. "I can't find Annie. Have you seen her?"

Thinking fast, Annie pointed toward the far side of the room. The instant Jason left, she cackled an excuse to Robyn and Nicole. Then she dashed through the crowd to meet Jason on the other side of the room.

It was going to be a very long night.

Returning from the refreshment table with a glass of cider and three pumpkin cookies, Dave saw Danielle Atron tap Vince on the shoulder.

"I'd like a word with you, Vince," Danielle Atron said with narrowed eyes. She was dressed like a flapper from the twenties with a close-fitting, gold cap on her head. The layers of fringe on her short, gold dress swished as she turned and walked away.

"Be right there, Ms. Atron." Vince gave his hand-held GC 161 detector to Dave. "Keep an eye on things until I get back."

"Problem, Vince?" Dave asked with a mouthful of cookie. Stuffing the other two cookies in his pocket, he took the small device.

"Maybe. Every kid in town is here, and we haven't detected a single molecule of GC 161." Squaring his shoulders, Vince turned to follow Danielle, then looked back. "If anything registers, come get me immediately."

"Right." After Vince left, Dave checked the control panel. The lights on the panel were connected to the lights on the detectors. All of them were green.

"She's too smart to walk into this stupid trap," Bobby said as he stepped up beside Dave.

"How would she know it's a trap?"

"She's a witch!" Bobby took the detector from Dave's hand and stared at it. "She knows you guys have a gadget that can blow her cover. So why would she deliberately come in here where you could catch her?"

"You've got a point." Dave nodded in agreement.

Vince was certain that the GC 161 kid and Bobby's witch were the same person. However, Bobby didn't know about the powerful chemical. The boy thought they really were looking for a witch.

"Yeah. She's out *there* somewhere." Bobby pointed through the corridor. He tightened his grip on the detector and motioned to his two friends. They marched in single file behind him as he headed toward the lobby.

"Where are you going, Bobby?" Dave called.

"To find the witch!"

Dave hesitated. Vince would be angry if he left the control panel, but Bobby was right. The witch was not at the party.

Dave ran after the boys, orange hair bouncing and his floppy, clown shoes flapping against the floor.

CHAPTER 9

Alex was bored to death. Groaning, she took off her hat and mask and stretched out on the back seat. She'd only been there fifteen minutes, but it felt like hours. She'd already finished the candy bar she took along from home, being careful to hide the wrapper under the seat so no one would know she'd been there.

Through the rear window, she could see the factory complex. Some sections shimmered under exterior lights. The shadowed parts blended into the dark sky. Spires and domes were linked by huge, twisting pipes, and hidden machinery thundered and hissed.

Ultra-creepy, Alex thought as her gaze drifted to the side window. She could see rows of shiny parked cars under the street lamps that lit the lot.

Shivering, Alex sat up and pressed her face against the glass. The lighted windows of the administration building gleamed in the distance. Inside, the employees of Paradise Valley Chemical and their families were enjoying Danielle Atron's generous hospitality. Only Alexandra Mack was absent, exiled to a car in a boring parking lot to spend Halloween night alone.

"Hey!" Alex exclaimed as she saw movement across the lot. It looked as if she wasn't alone and the parking lot wasn't deserted!

A Rocket Ranger in a white helmet walked under one of the street lamps on the left.

Alex ducked, then raised herself just enough to peer outside. Another small, dark figure was walking right toward her. An orange lightning bolt and a black mask were clearly visible as Bobby Barnswell walked into a circle of light. He was holding a small, black thing that looked like a remote control. A green light shone from it.

The GC 161 detector!

Alex ducked again and stayed ducked. When Bobby walked by the family car, the GC 161 in her system would trigger the device and the light would turn red.

Alex brought her knees up to her chest and scrunched into a ball. Then she thought about the grim reality of her situation.

The kid would have his witch.

Vince and Danielle would have their GC 161 accident victim.

And life as a normal, junior high kid would be lost to Alex forever.

But Alex had no intention of letting *that* happen. Even though she had powers that *weren't* normal, she was still a fourteen-year-old girl who wanted to go to school and hang out with her friends just like everyone else.

Looping the flexible witch mask through her rope belt, Alex put on her hat. A wooded park bordered the remote end of the parking lot. Hoping to disappear into the trees, she quietly opened the door and slipped outside.

"Yeow!" A boy yelled.

Startled, Alex let go of the door and it banged closed.

"What was that?" Bobby looked up sharply. "Howard?"

Alex crept to the back of the car and crouched down low beneath the trunk.

"I stubbed my toe!" the first boy yelled.

"No, I mean the car!" Bobby scanned the parking lot. "I heard a car door slam."

"Where?" The third boy came running.

"I'm not sure, Greg." Bobby threw up his hands in frustration. "It could have come from anywhere."

Another bit of luck, Alex thought. At least Bobby couldn't connect her with the Mack's family car. But she had to get away from it and find a better place to hide.

"Let's split up again," Bobby suggested.

Alex waited as Howard and Greg took off in opposite directions. Then she eased backward and turned toward the woods.

"Find something, Bobby?" Another, older voice called out.

Dave! Alex stopped abruptly, and her heart skipped a beat. Anxious to put some distance between herself and Bobby's posse, Alex scurried between two cars, across a lane, and between two more cars. She set a course through the dark areas, where the lights didn't reach. She couldn't be seen, but she couldn't see very well, either. She tripped over a pothole and sprawled on the pavement just as one of Bobby's friends rounded the corner.

"There she is! Bobby! Greg! Over here!"

Scrambling to her feet, Alex darted toward the cars in front of her. *Bad move,* she realized as Howard directed the other Rangers' movements.

"Over there, Greg! Head her off. She's right in front of you, Bobby. We've got her surrounded."

"I see her!" Bobby shouted and ran toward her from behind.

Alex turned right. There was barely enough room to squeeze between the front bumpers of the parked cars. When Alex entered the next dark area, she paused. She had to morph to elude her pursuers, but being slightly winded and surrounded by Rocket Rangers made the transformation process harder. Closing her eyes, she concentrated on her toes. A warm prickling spread through her feet and up her legs with the speed of a sluggish snail.

"Where'd she go?" Dave asked.

"Don't know," Bobby said, "but she's in this row somewhere. We'll find her."

The boys were closing in.

Focusing her energies, Alex suddenly felt a surge of heat flood her body. A hot shivering sensation swept through her as she transformed from solid into fluid.

As a puddle, Alex slithered under the cars, across the cold and scratchy pavement. Reaching the last car in the row, she paused to consider her options.

Playing possum as a puddle would be easy, except for one thing. The transformation process took a lot of energy, and she couldn't stay in her liquid state for more than five minutes. Not yet anyway. Her stamina was improving, but whether she wanted to or not, she would rematerialize soon. And she couldn't take the chance that one of the boys or Dave might see her do it!

Alex peeked out from under the car. The factory was just ahead, surrounded by a high fence and separated from the parking lot by a stretch of lawn. A short distance behind her, the boys and Dave were searching around every car. If she changed back to her normal self and made a run for it, they'd see her. Still, she'd have a head start and there were plenty of places to hide in the complex . . . if she could find a way inside.

Sliding out from under the car, Alex changed into her solid self and bolted toward the factory.

"There she goes!" Greg cried out.

"She can't get away from us now!" Bobby said confidently.

Alex didn't look back. She hit the grass at a dead run, completely focused on reaching safety in the industrial maze.

The chainlink fence was topped by three rows of slanted, barbed wire to prevent anyone from climbing over. Hoping to find a gate, Alex angled to the right. She raced around the corner of the fence just as the boys and Dave reached the grass.

Down the length of the fence, Alex spotted a gate. Rushing toward it, she realized it had an electronic lock that was connected to an alarm. The high-tech security equipment might prevent an ordinary person from breaking into the complex, but opening an electronic device was a piece of cake for Alex Mack, the human zapper.

The boys charged toward the corner. Moving close to the gate control panel, Alex positioned herself to shield the zapper's flash. A stream of electrical energy shot from her fingers. After short-circuiting the alarm, she disengaged the lock. A split second later, she was through the gate and out of sight behind a wall of monster pipes.

Alex paused to catch her breath, but the boys had been gaining on her steadily. Too tired to morph again right away, she dropped to the ground and rolled under a metal ledge as they dashed through the gate.

Bobby skidded to a halt where the conduits began, holding the detector in front of him. His mask hung around his neck by an elastic string. He frowned.

Huffing and puffing, Dave stopped behind him.

Alex clamped her hand over her mouth. In his blue and white clown suit with a ruffled, yellow collar and yellow pom poms down the front, Dave looked so comical, she almost laughed. In fact, if the circumstances hadn't been so dangerous, the whole scenario would be laughable. It wasn't every day three Rocket Rangers and a clown chased a witch through a chemical plant.

"Got something?" Dave asked.

"Nothing." Bobby shook the device and frowned. "How close do I have to be for this thing to work?"

"Ten feet, I think," Dave said.

Ten feet, Alex thought. That was definitely a good thing to know.

"Hey, Bobby!" Howard called from the far end of the narrow corridor. "We lost her again."

"And we'll find her again!" Staring at the detector, Bobby started toward Alex's position.

Dave hung back. "Guess I'd better call Vince. He'll be *really* mad if I don't tell him someone broke into the plant."

Alex scrambled through an opening into another, smaller corridor lined with smaller pipes. More pipes connected by valves and odd-shaped joints formed a low ceiling overhead. The cramped passageway led into the main complex.

There were a million hiding places in the factory, and the party would be over in a couple of hours. If she could stay out of sight and out of the detector's range, she would be safe until it was time to go home.

Once inside, Alex moved quickly through the chemical production facility. The graveyard shift had been cut to a skeleton crew so most of the workers could attend the party. She easily avoided the few technicians scattered throughout the industrial plant. However, the Rocket Rangers were proving to be very difficult to lose.

"Yo, Bobby!" Greg's voice echoed through the huge installation. "Where are you?"

"Over here!" Bobby shouted back.

"Vince is on his way!" Dave called from another direction. "Where are you guys?"

Afraid of being surrounded again, Alex decided to go up. She climbed a metal stairway to a network of metal ramps, moving slowly so her footsteps would not be heard.

The walkways skirted an open area filled with pipes and machinery. Pipes of various sizes were anchored to the floor thirty feet below and connected with a tangle of pipes, cables, and valves on the ceiling high above.

As Alex stepped onto the high ramp, she paused to search the lower level for the boys. The only thing between her and a deadly fall was a thin, metal railing. Machines with sharp edges and spikes, moving levers and gears filled the main floor. Suddenly dizzy, she staggered backward and clutched the railing. The loose, metal bar rattled, and the sound was amplified in the cavernous complex.

"That you, Bobby?" Dave called from below. "You guys shouldn't be up there! It's too dangerous."

Angry with herself for being so careless, Alex darted around the deep opening to the dense maze of pipes and machinery on the far side. She ducked into a dark space between flattened, vertical pipes and prepared to morph.

"Bobby?" Dave's voice rang out and his large, floppy shoes clattered on the stairs.

Alex glanced out as Dave reached the top of the stairs and took a step toward the metal ramp. The tip of his long clown shoe caught on the ramp, tripping him. He fell against the loose railing and the metal bar broke. Yellow pom poms and orange hair fluttered as he frantically waved his arms, but he couldn't keep his balance.

Alex watched in horror as Dave toppled off the ramp with a chilling scream.

CHAPTER 10

Alex exhaled in relief as Dave miraculously managed to grab onto one of the pipes that stretched from floor to ceiling. He wrapped his arms and legs around the pipe, then his red nose popped off. The red ball hit a bank of levers on the floor, then ricocheted around the machinery.

"Help! Someone! Help!" Dave shouted.

"What's the matter, Dave?" Bobby yelled.

"Up here!" Dave cried, still wrapped tightly around the pipe.

"Don't move, Dave!" Vince ordered sharply. "I'm coming."

Suddenly the pipe Dave was clinging to creaked and leaned slightly. Alex gasped.

"Better hurry, Vince," Dave pleaded. A startled cry escaped him as the pipe jerked and leaned a little more.

Alex's gaze traveled to the pipe-joint a few feet above Dave's head. She saw that the pipe was breaking free of the connection.

Vince and Bobby's posse raced up the stairs to the rescue.

Dangling thirty feet in the air, Dave closed his eyes and tightened his grip.

Alex hesitated. If she morphed now, while everyone was distracted by Dave's dangerous situation, she could easily escape into the labyrinth of equipment and conduits. She might even make it back outside, something the witch-hunters wouldn't expect. They'd keep searching for her inside the complex while she hid in the trees and waited for her family.

The metal joint groaned and bent. Dave's pipe fell a few more inches.

"Vince!" Dave shrieked.

But Vince would not reach the landing in time to save Dave from a lethal plunge to the floor, Alex realized. She could save herself or Dave. She didn't even have to think about it. She could not let the man fall to his death.

The joint snapped. The pipe and Dave began to plummet. Dave cried out in fear.

Alex reacted instantly. As the pipe continued to drop, she slowed its downward motion with the force of her mind. The combined weight of the man and the long, metal pipe took her by surprise. She had never tried using telekinesis on anything so heavy before, and she lost her hold for a split second. The pipe continued to fall toward the ground.

Dave's grip slipped. He hung on, but he would not be able to cling to the pipe much longer.

Drawing on an inner reserve, Alex summoned the enormous energies she needed to move the pipe back toward the broken joint. Beads of sweat broke out on her face as she concentrated on the pipe. Her whole body went rigid with the effort, but the pipe slowly moved back.

Dave's eyes were still shut in anticipation of a fall, and he was not aware of the pipe's awesome ability to defy gravity. The end of the pipe clicked back into the broken joint just as Vince and the boys scrambled onto the landing.

"Hold on, Dave!" Vince was pale and his voice

shook slightly as he reached for a lever by the stairs. "Don't lose it now!"

Dave held on.

But Alex almost lost it. The physical drain was steadily weakening her telekinetic ability.

Vince flipped the lever and a mechanism whirred. A metal panel swung outward in an arc from under the ramp. It connected with the ramp on Alex's side of the opening to create a bridge.

Hurry, Vince! Alex trembled as the security man rushed onto the bridge. She was running out of strength. Although Dave was suspended a mere two feet from the new ramp, he didn't move. He was still terrified.

Vince reached out and grabbed Dave around the waist. Dave squealed as Vince pulled him to safety on the bridge.

Alex released the pipe. It fell, landing with a clattering crash that resounded throughout the complex.

Collapsing in an exhausted heap, Alex watched and listened while she tried to regain her depleted strength. If they started searching for her again now, before she had recovered enough to morph, she'd be in major trouble.

The truck driver's eyes popped open and he

touched his chest, as though he couldn't quite believe he had survived the ordeal. "Vince! You saved my life! How can I ever thank—"

"Don't get carried away, Dave," Vince said in his normal clipped, sarcastic tone. Stepping back, he straightened his tie and jacket self-consciously. "I *had* to save you. You're the only one who saw that kid, remember?"

"Yeah, right." Dave grinned. "What about Bobby? He's a witness, too."

"He's a kid who thinks he saw a witch." Vince threw up his hands. "I mean, give me a break. Glowing eyes and warts? For all I know, he made the whole thing up."

"I did not!" Bobby's eyes flashed with indignation.

Rolling his eyes, Vince started back toward the main ramp. "Calm down, kid. It's not a problem, okay? Everyone gets a little spooked on Halloween."

"I'll show you!" With the detector firmly in hand, Bobby moved down the ramp. "She's in here, and I'm gonna find her."

Alex edged back as far as she could before an intersecting bank of pipes stopped her. Bobby would be within ten feet of her position within seconds! Desperate, she tried to morph. All she managed was a slight quivering that created ripples in her skin.

"Listen, kid," Vince said impatiently. "I'm sorry I doubted you, okay? Now get back here. That device is a valuable piece of equipment—"

"It's red!" Bobby stared at the glowing readout, his eyes wide and his mouth open. "The light just turned red!"

Caught!

Alex felt the blood drain from her face. She had to save herself now, and she had to act fast. Bobby was standing just beyond the opening into the dark, narrow space. He hadn't seen her—yet.

"Let me see that!" Vince's footsteps rattled the metal ramp as he hurried toward Bobby.

"She's gotta be hiding in these machines...." Bobby muttered, ignoring Vince's order.

Okay, Bobby, Alex thought with a surge of desperate inspiration. Like Danielle, who would never give up searching for the GC 161 kid, Bobby was becoming a real problem. *You want to find a witch? I'll give you a witch.*

Alex put on the witch mask and replaced her hat. She didn't know if she could get herself out of this mess, but she certainly wasn't going to surrender without a fight. A rush of anger sent a jolt of adrenaline through her system, renewing her strength. Supercharged and determined, Alex crept forward.

Bobby still held the detector at arm's length. Ready and waiting when it appeared in front of the opening, Alex let fly with a golden zapper. The electrical bolt struck the device, and Bobby dropped it with a squeal of alarm. It broke into pieces on the metal floor.

"Better watch out, Bobby." Alex cackled softly as the boy leaned over to stare at the destroyed device. Hidden in the shadows, she could not be seen clearly.

Bobby turned his head to peer into the space.

"Or I'll turn you into a toad. Heh, heh, heh . . ." Alex eased back into the dark. "I like toads . . . for breakfast!" When she reached the intersecting pipes, she cackled again. The quiet, witchy chuckle became a spooky gurgle as she slowly shifted into liquid form.

Bobby's eyes widened in horrified fascination.

"What the—" Vince stopped beside the boy and looked at the demolished detector. "I told you to be careful!"

"She melted!" Bobby gasped.

"What?" Vince asked uncertainly.

"The witch! She just melted into a puddle of slime and disappeared!"

"Melted and disappeared?" Vince hesitated. "You're sure?"

"Positive. I am *not* spooked because it's Halloween. I saw her with my own two eyes!"

"I believe you." Pulling a cellular phone out of his pocket, Vince called security. He ordered his guards to supply themselves with hand held detectors and surround the factory complex. Then he turned back to Bobby.

"Good job, kid. She's isolated and trapped, now. Maybe we can trace her through this maze. If not, we'll catch her when she tries to leave . . . even if she is a puddle."

Oozing between tightly stacked pipes, Alex fled in terror.

CHAPTER 11

After slithering around valves and between pipes for a couple of minutes, Alex knew she was lost. Worse. Even if she found an exit from the factory, a security team was waiting for her to emerge. The factory was surrounded, and Alex would have to solidify soon.

She entered a ventilation duct and headed down. The shaft seemed to go on forever, then finally joined with the main, horizontal duct. It was big enough for her to crawl in on hands and knees. Alex paused and materialized into her normal body. Then she looked around to get her bearings.

Blasts of heated air moved through the ventilation system. Sweating under the plastic mask, Alex took it off and tucked it into her belt.

Light shone through a grate just ahead. Crawling toward it, Alex prepared to morph and flee if someone was nearby with a detector. She expected to look out into the ground floor of the complex. Instead, the grate opened into a storage room. The only way out was through a heavy security door. She decided to stay in the ventilation network until she reached a familiar area.

Morphing again, Alex sped through the main duct. The few grates she encountered all opened into secured storage rooms. When the duct dead-ended, she backtracked and turned into the first vertical shaft. Moving upward on smooth metal might have been impossible, but the bolted seams where the sections joined provided just enough traction. As she turned into the next horizontal duct, she heard music and people laughing. Alex hurried toward a lighted grate. Beyond it, the employee Halloween party was in full swing.

Materializing, Alex stretched out on her stomach. Apparently, the main duct ran underground between the industrial complex and the administration building. By accident she had found the party and escaped Vince's guards!

Safe for the moment, Alex propped her chin in her hands. Her mom and dad were dancing to "The Monster Mash," and Annie was sitting at a table with Jason. Robyn was talking to a boy with bandages wrapped around his head and arms—a mummy wearing a T-shirt, torn jeans, and sneakers. Nicole laughed, cheering on a werewolf bobbing for apples. She looked really pretty in the gypsy costume. Then Alex saw Scott and her heart fluttered. He was an absolutely awesome Robin Hood.

It just isn't fair, Alex thought miserably. Everyone in town was having a great time, and she was sitting in a stupid air-duct. Then she saw Raymond and had an idea.

Although Vince was hunting for her with more determination than ever, his search was focused on the factory. The party was the *last* place he'd expect to find her. Maybe she wouldn't have to miss all the fun!

The grate was in the wall by the refreshment table, and Raymond was headed right for it. All the GC 161 detectors were at the entrance on the far side of the room. As long as she didn't go near them, everything would be fine.

If she could get into the room without being seen.

"Pssst! Raymond!" Alex whispered as loud as she dared.

"Huh? What?" Raymond stopped and glanced over his shoulder.

"Down here! It's me. Alex."

Dropping on one knee, Raymond peered through the wire covering. "What are you doing in there? You were supposed to wait in the car."

"I'll explain later, Raymond. It's a long story. Right now, I need you to stand in front of this grate so I can get out."

"Okay. I hope you know what you're doing."

Hidden from view by Raymond's cape, Alex morphed and slid under the grate. Within seconds, she was her solid self again. "Thanks, Raymond."

"I'm not sure I did you any favors, Alex. Those detectors—"

"—are over there, and I'm over here." Alex grinned sheepishly. "And speaking of favors . . . I need another one."

"I'm afraid to ask."

"Go to the car and get my broom. Please. You can sneak it in under your cape."

"Yeah, sure." Raymond smiled. "I don't know what you've been up to, but I'm glad you're all right." Closing his cape with a dramatic sweep of his arms, Raymond left.

And Scott walked over. "Hey, Alex. Got tired of the weird witch routine, huh?" Alex wasn't wearing her mask.

"Uh—yeah." Alex shrugged, wondering just how weird Annie's performance had been. "It was fun for a while, but pretending to be a cranky old witch can be a drag at a party."

"Yeah, I guess." Scott's brown eyes sparkled. "But you were such a cute cranky old witch."

"Really?" Alex blushed.

Just then Kelly showed up.

"Well, if it isn't the Wicked Witch of the East." Dressed as Maid Marian in an elegant gown with a jeweled headband, Kelly looked beautiful. She hooked her arm through Scott's.

"Be nice, Kelly," Scott said, trying to take the sting out of the confrontation. "Or she'll cast an evil spell over you."

"She already threatened to turn me into a toad once tonight."

Way to go, Annie! Alex thought. She met Kelly's superior stare, imagining her as a brown toad with a tiny headband and gown.

"C'mon, Scott. Let's dance."

"Catch ya later, Alex," Scott said as Kelly dragged him toward the dance floor.

"Right." Sighing, Alex turned and found herself standing nose-to-nose with Annie.

"What are you doing here?" Annie demanded. Standing with one hand planted on her hip and holding a broom in the other, Annie tapped her foot in angry agitation. Her hat was on crooked and the point flopped over. She looked ridiculous, and Alex giggled.

"This is not funny, Alex," Annie said in a low, serious tone. "I've been going crazy all night trying to remember which one of us I'm supposed to be! I'm sure your friends are really cool for eighth graders, but hanging out with them has been a major pain. And Jason probably thinks I'm a total scatterbrain because I keep making lame excuses so I can disappear to be you for a while. And now—here you are!"

"I'm sorry, Annie. I couldn't help it. Bobby Barnswell decided to search the parking lot with a detector." Drawing Annie into a corner for privacy, Alex filled her in on the details.

"Doesn't anything ever go right for you, Alex?"

"Well, they're not looking for me here. It could be worse."

"It is," Annie said simply. "When the party's over, how are you going to get past the detectors to leave?"

"The same way I got in!" Alex brightened.

"I don't think so."

Alex followed Annie's gaze to the entrance. Vince, Dave, the Rocket Rangers, and six guards carrying detectors entered. The uniformed security people moved to strategic spots throughout the room. A stern-looking, muscular woman planted herself in front of the ventilation grate. There was no way out.

"I know Halloween is supposed to be a frightening experience, but this is ridiculous," Annie said.

CHAPTER 12

Alex stood in the middle of the room, as far away as she could get from the detector-bearing guards spaced along the walls. Vince was talking with Danielle Atron by the entrance, and Dave was watching the control panel. Bobby and the Rocket Rangers had apparently lost interest in the witch hunt. The boys were engrossed in an animated discussion with a group of friends.

"Here you go, Alex." Raymond held out a soda, then slipped the broom out from under his cape and into Alex's hand.

"Thanks." Clutching the broom, Alex sipped the soda and looked nervously around the room.

"Try to look like you're having a good time," Annie said.

"Easy for you to say. You're not going to end up as Danielle Atron's door prize by midnight," Alex pointed out.

"Maybe you could just zap all the detectors," Raymond suggested. "They won't work if they're broken."

"Danielle would just make more," Annie said grimly. "They work perfectly, and she can install them anywhere she wants. Alex is the only kid in town with GC 161 in her system. Eventually, they'd find her."

Alex paled. She hadn't thought about the far-reaching implications of the new detector. Danielle could hang them in the school, at the mall—even on street corners, and Alex would never know when she might be within range.

"I won't be able to leave the house!"

"Not unless we think of something." Annie sighed heavily. "I'm working on it."

Alex did not recall ever seeing Annie quite so perplexed by a problem. Her spirits sank impossibly lower.

Just then Jason rushed over and gently took Annie's arm. "C'mon. They're going to announce the winners in the costume contest."

"But we didn't enter the contest," Annie protested.

"The judges have been circulating all night," Jason explained. "Everyone's in it."

The crowd surged forward, sweeping Alex along with it. Boxed in, she frantically looked toward the guards flanking the stage. They seemed to be more than ten feet away on either side, and she tried to relax. If she started glowing now, Vince wouldn't need a detector to I.D. her.

"Okay, ghosts and ghouls!" The deejay palmed a microphone. "We have our winners!"

Danielle Atron stood off to the side, surveying her employees with a regal smile. Vince stood behind her. He was not smiling.

"Best couple!" The deejay paused, then pointed toward the audience. "Robin Hood and Maid Marian!"

Alex clapped absently. Her attention was not on the awards. Something nagged at the back of her mind. Something Annie said had planted the seeds of an idea she couldn't quite grasp. There was a way to defeat the detectors . . . not just for now, but forever. *How?*

"Yo, Alex!" Grinning, Nicole waved. The werewolf beside her bared fake fangs and howled.

Alex waved back, then forced a smile as Robyn left the teenaged mummy and edged toward her through the crowd.

"How's it going, Alex? You've been kinda quiet the past hour or so. You're not still sick, are you?"

"No, I'm fine." Alex nodded, then blinked when the deejay called her name.

"Alex and Annie Mack! The twin witches of Paradise Valley. C'mon up here, girls!"

"Right on, Alex!" Raymond urged her gently toward the stage.

Annie took a step backward, shaking her head. "No way. I'm not going up there and making a spectacle of myself."

"Don't be shy, Annie," Jason said. "You guys put on a great act! You deserve to win something."

Alex balked too, but there was no way to avoid the unwanted attention.

"C'mon, Alex," Annie said. "Let's get this over with. The steps are in the middle. Just stay close to center stage and you'll be okay."

Nodding, Alex followed Annie onto the platform in a daze. She barely heard what the deejay was saying as she stared into the sea of masked and painted faces before her. Expecting Vince to come charging forward with the detector any second, she stiffened when the deejay edged between her and Annie.

". . . proud to present the Spirit of Halloween Award to Alex and Annie Mack." The deejay handed Annie a plaque and gave Alex a check for fifty dollars. "Congratulations. Let's hear it for these enthusiastic performers, folks. They put on a great show!" Clapping, the deejay stepped aside.

Annie bowed stiffly, then nudged Alex to move.

Applause and cheers thundered in Alex's ears, shattering her paralysis. No one knew she had not been at the party all night! And being on stage now, side by side with Annie, proved it beyond doubt! She glanced at Danielle Atron.

The woman was clapping halfheartedly with a bored expression. Vince whispered something to her. She dismissed him with an annoyed wave. Vince hesitated, then headed back to the entrance.

Danielle Atron was upset. Why? The detectors worked perfectly. . . .

"Move, Alex!" Annie hissed.

"I've got it!" Laughing, Alex hurried off the stage. She and Annie were immediately mobbed by their friends.

"This is so cool!" Raymond held up the plaque.

"What are you gonna do with the money?" Robyn asked.

"I'm so proud of you!" Mrs. Mack kissed Alex on the cheek and Mr. Mack vigorously shook Annie's hand.

Bobby Barnswell zeroed in on Alex. "Do I know you?"

"Not really," Alex said evenly. Bobby had never gotten a good look at his witch, but he had seen *her* clearly once, without the costume. "I answered the door when you came to my house trick-or-treating."

"Oh, yeah. I knew I'd seen you somewhere."

"Did you finish your mission?" Alex couldn't resist asking.

Sagging, Bobby shook his head. "No, but this is one Halloween I won't ever forget. At least I'll finish grade school as a boy and not a toad!"

Alex smiled as Bobby left. One problem solved. One to go.

"Congratulations, Alex." Scott extended his hand, but before Alex could shake it, Annie whisked her aside, ignoring her protests.

"Mom and Dad want to leave soon, and—" Annie paused to take a deep breath. "I'm sorry,

Alex, but I don't have a clue how to get you out of here without triggering those devices."

"But I do." Alex explained in an excited rush. "As far as Danielle Atron and Vince are concerned, everyone at this party got in without setting off the detectors . . . including me, right?"

"Right . . ." Annie stared at her, confused at first, then curious.

"And Vince knows that the handheld detector was triggered in the theater. But when he reset it, it didn't turn red again because I was already gone. Then Bobby's detector flashed red in the factory and he didn't find anyone there, either."

"So?"

"So maybe we can convince him that the detectors are faulty. If Danielle thinks they don't work, she won't make any more and I won't have to worry about them."

"A good idea in theory, Alex, but I don't see how—"

"The detectors stayed green when everyone came in." Alex interrupted. "What if they all flash red when everyone leaves? That would prove the device isn't reliable, wouldn't it?"

Annie blinked, then blinked again. "Yes. Yes, it would."

"And," Alex finished triumphantly, "I can make it happen using my powers."

"Well, we'd better get started." Annie nodded toward the entrance. "Everyone's getting ready to go home."

In order to figure out the triggering mechanism, Alex had to set off the detector first. With Annie and Raymond following, Alex crossed the room and paused just out of detector range. She didn't want to set off the devices too soon.

As the first group of people reached the exit, Alex moved closer. The detectors responded to the GC 161 in her system.

"It's red, Vince!" Dave shouted excitedly. "It's red."

Alex smiled. The light operated on a simple switch she could easily manipulate with her telekinetic power.

Vince immediately halted the employees lined up to leave through the narrow passageway. Then he reset the detectors to green.

"Okay, folks," Vince barked. "One at a time, please. No need to rush."

A tall man passed by first, and Alex triggered the red light.

"Stand over there." Vince reset the device, then

looked up. The man frowned, but he stepped aside as ordered. No one wanted to argue with Vince.

"But we're looking for a kid, Vince," Dave said.

"I know that!" Vince snapped. "Next!"

A dozen people walked by and set off the detectors. Vince detained them all until Danielle Atron finally intervened.

"Go on home, people." Danielle waved everyone through the haunted house exit with a warm smile. "Just a malfunction of the security system. Thank you for coming."

Standing off to the side with Annie and Raymond, Alex continued to turn the lights red.

"Forget it, Vince!" Ms. Atron stormed toward him.

"They worked perfectly in the labs," Vince insisted as he frantically continued to reset the detectors.

"Then there must be something wrong with our testing techniques." Danielle's voice had a sharp edge and her eyes flashed angrily as she pushed Vince out of the way.

"Something very odd is going on here, Ms. Atron," Vince said. "This device works."

"Wrong. *This* was a complete waste of time and

money." Danielle picked up the control panel and smashed it on the floor.

Alex almost laughed out loud as bits of electronic components sputtered and sparked, then sizzled into silence. The lights on the detectors in the passageway blinked green and red, then went dark.

Turning with a swish of gold fringe, Danielle Atron cast a withering glance at Vince. "Don't forget to lock up."

Dave sidled up to Vince and grinned. "Guess we're still partners, huh?"

"Don't remind me." Vince stomped on the broken control panel and left.

Annie sighed with relief. "Let's get out of here."

"I'll see ya tomorrow," Raymond said. "I've gotta help my Dad clean up."

Alex tensed as she went through the passageway. Although the implanted detectors remained dark, the elborate trap was a reminder of Danielle Atron's determination. She would never give up trying to identify Alex, but at least she wouldn't be using the detectors to do it.

"Thanks for everything you did for me tonight, Annie," Alex said as they walked across the parking lot toward the car. "It wasn't easy being both of us."

"To be honest, it was kind of fun."

"I'm glad you had a good time," Alex said.

"Yeah, I did. As it turns out, Jason's really nice." Annie held out the plaque and cocked her head. "Although winning the Spirit of Halloween Award is a dubious distinction at best."

Alex handed Annie the check. "Here. You did all the work. Besides, you'll probably spend it on stuff you need for your pet science project anyway."

"You? You're probably right. How else am I going to win a Nobel Prize without you to experiment on?"

"True." Alex grinned. Although Annie would rarely admit it, she really was more interested in Alex's welfare than in achieving scientific fame and fortune.

"Although, maybe you've got more of the Mack scientific genius than you realize, Alex," Annie said. "Turning the detector lights red to discredit the technology was a brilliant idea. Now, Danielle Atron thinks the detectors are completely worthless."

The satisfaction Alex felt at outsmarting Danielle

Atron was nothing compared to the sense of pride she got from Annie's praise.

"You inspired me, Annie." Then Alex had another inspired idea. She glanced around the dark, remote corner of the parking lot. No one was in sight, and she swung her leg over the witch's broom. "Think I can make this thing fly?"

Annie panicked. "No. Don't, Alex. Someone might see—"

Straddling the broom, Alex concentrated. She rose a whole six inches off the ground before she lost it and fell on the pavement. "Trick or treat!"

"Some trick!" Grinning, Annie helped Alex to her feet. "For a second there, I actually thought you could do it!"

"Oh, I'm gonna work on it," Alex said, tucking the broom under her arm. "You thought this Halloween was scary! Just wait till next year!"

About The Author

Diana G. Gallagher lives in Kansas with her husband, Marty Burke, two dogs, three cats, and a cranky parrot. When she's not writing, she likes to read and take long walks with the dogs.

A Hugo Award-winning illustrator, she is best known for her series *Woof: The House Dragon.* Her songs about humanity's future are sung throughout the world and have been recorded in cassette form: "Cosmic Concepts More Complete," "Star*Song," and "Fire Dream." Diana and Marty, an Irish folksinger, perform traditional and original music at science-fiction conventions.

Her first adult novel, *The Alien Dark,* appeared in 1990. She is also the author of a *Star Trek: Deep Space Nine*® novel for young readers, *Arcade,* and two other books in *The Secret World of Alex Mack* series, all available from Minstrel Books.

She is currently working on another *Star Trek* novel and a new *Alex Mack* story.